A HOME FOR NOEL

Rachel Lopez

rachelrlopez.com

For information contact:
Synecdoche Publishing
synecdochepublishing.wordpress.com

Edited by Jill Monday and Mary Luce
Book design by Amanda Hovseth
Cover by NoirCat Designs

ISBN: 978-1-945018-19-0 (soft cover); 978-1-945018-20-6 (eBook)

Library of Congress Control Number:

First Edition: 2019

DEDICATION

I dedicate this book to anyone who has been
a beacon of light for those in need. Your choice to
give selflessly matters, and you change lives.

CHAPTER ONE

Christmas 1999

The breaking of glass followed by a scream of anguish rent the air. Jesse almost turned back right then, but Noel saw him coming. Not to mention, his mother would pepper him with questions if he didn't bring her back with him. He didn't lie well enough to be dishonest – especially to his mother–she'd see right through him.

Noel Miracle sat perched upon the saggy wooden porch littered with garbage and rusty appliances, her dirty face tear-streaked. Amid all the trash, garbage, and green-stained vinyl siding, she was the most beautiful girl Jesse had ever laid eyes on. Like an angel in the middle of a battlefield.

"Hey," Jessie said when he got close enough to be heard over the fighting that raged from inside the Miracle home. Shyly, he looked down at his new shoes. The fancy sneakers were now covered in snow but still very warm and dry–a gift from Santa that very morning.

"Hi Jesse," Noel's gray eyes lit up as he approached. Jesse Wellings was her favorite person in the entire world. He and his family protected her.

"Merry Christmas," Jesse said. His voice barely audible over the harsh words floating from inside the Miracle's home.

"Oh yes, Merry Christmas," Noel's shoulders sagged, her large eyes filled with fresh tears as she realized that Santa had forgotten her.

With insight far beyond his nine years, Jesse chose not to ask how her

1

morning had gone. Instead he asked, "You wanna come to my house?"

Nervously, Noel glanced back at her home The shabby wooden planks on the white washed home rattled as a door slammed somewhere in the back. Wiping her eyes with the back of her bare arm, she nodded her head, her dirty platinum locks falling into her face.

"What are we gonna do?" She asked, her small voice raspy from the constant exposure to cigarette smoke in her home.

"Mom wants to know if you'll have Christmas dinner with us?" Jesse's cheeks reddened.

"Get out, trash!" An explosion of splintering glass banged against the inner walls making Jesse jump. Taking two steps back, he was ready to bolt.

"You'd be begging me to stay before I pulled out of the drive," Mr. Miracle growled.

"Fat chance of that! I don't need you. Go on, I'll be fine without you!" The sound of heavy objects being tossed inside was enough for the young pair.

"Let's go." Noel lept from the porch. Grabbing Jesse's arm–nearly pulling his shoulder out of socket–she led the way to the Wellings home.

The fighting had just started, and history told Noel it would get much worse before either of her parents simmered down. The chances of a truce before sundown was unlikely.

"Do...do you need to tell someone?" Jesse glanced back at her home praying Mr. Miracle wouldn't come outside. The man frightened him terribly.

She shook her head, "They won't even notice I'm gone."

Once again, Jesse remained silent. Noel released his arm and skipped ahead of him, the prospect of a good meal driving thoughts of Santa and her parents from her mind.

CHAPTER TWO

The mixed scent of holiday foods hit Noel's tiny body in a wave of delicious warmth. Taking in a deep breath of the delectable smells, Noel decided she had just entered heaven or the earthly equivalent of it. Her cold arms and legs began to thaw. Jesse motioned for her to follow him into the kitchen.

Noel knew where they headed-through the festively decorated dining room and straight into the kitchen to see Jana Wellings. Jana loved Noel, and Noel loved her right back.

"Oh Noel! I'm so happy you made it sweetheart. Come in, come in dear." Jana's heart crushed after one look at the child who wore clothing unsuitable for winter. *How had she not frozen to death?* Jana thought. "Oh sweetie, you look cold, go in the family room and sit near the fire. Dinner will be later this evening, but I can make a snack for you and Jesse if you'd like."

Mrs. Wellings kind face lit up when she looked at the sweet girl. Her ever watchful eyes, looked Noel's thin frame over, she fought back the urge to go down the road and give the Miracles a piece of her mind. How could anyone look at that child and not just melt?

"I can wait until dinner, thank you," the child answered politely. She reached out to hug Mrs. Wellings plump frame, the woman returned the

3

embrace pouring as much love as she could into that small act of affection. The child was starved for attention.

Mrs. Wellings puckered her mouth for a moment, "Well, at least have a cup of my famous hot chocolate, that'll warm you right up."

Noel pulled back, a smile lighting up her sweet face. It'd been ages since she had anything sweet. It had been ages since she had real food at all. Christmas break was the worst, her school gave her a bag of snacks for the break, but those had long since been eaten. Now, she ate whatever canned garbage her mother thought to buy at the nearest liquor store–during her daily alcohol run. That's to say, *when* Mrs. Miracle remembered to pick up any food at all.

"Thank you," Noel smiled.

She loved Mrs. Wellings, her wrinkled face radiated love and a joy that lit up the room. She was pretty for a woman of her age, her silver hair always stylishly cut, and her outfits made of fine materials. She was a curvy woman, but Noel thought it made for the best kind of hugs.

Jana Wellings was the opposite of Noel's mother who wore the same clothes days on end. Her mother rarely brushed her hair let alone cut or styled it. When she was home alone, Noel pretended to be Mrs. Wellings, fixing her hair to the best of her ability. Sometimes, she even used what little makeup her mother had trying to mimic the woman's classy look.

"Jess help me in the kitchen please," Mrs. Wellings directed. "Noel go sit by the fire and turn on some cartoons sweetie. Jesse will bring your cocoa to you."

"Yes, ma'am," she said eager for the fire and the cocoa.

The walk from her home to the Wellings wasn't long, but she felt frozen all the way to her bones. *I should be used to it by now,* she thought. She hadn't had a proper coat for two years. The lack of protection from the cold made for miserable walks on snowy Christmas days.

"Were they at it again?" Mrs. Wellings asked once the girl was out of earshot.

"Yes, Mr. Miracle said he was leaving, they were throwing stuff and cursing. It was awful." Jesse shuddered at the thought of living in a home like that.

Mrs. Wellings listened to her son as she prepared two steaming mugs of hot chocolate; her secret recipe, topped with a mound of snowman shaped marshmallows.

"The poor dear–" she said shaking her head.

"And it's like she forgot it's Christmas or something! I wished her a Merry Christmas, and she got this blank look on her face for a minute. Then tears started flowing down her cheeks. I didn't know what to say." Jesse's innocent eyes opened wide in confusion.

"Insufferable...cruel," Mrs. Wellings mumbled. She understood all too well that liquor consumed the Miracle's lives, robbing Noel of her childhood. Her mind drifted to the baby doll and stroller wrapped inside her closet for the girl.

"Do you think Santa was too scared of Mr. Miracle to bring Noel her presents, and that's why she forgot it was Christmas?" Jesse asked his faith in Santa dwindling.

"I don't...know...Jess, can you and Noel go out back and help your daddy bring more firewood in? I have to run to the drugstore and get...something I forgot." Mrs. Wellings asked distractedly.

"Yes Momma, can we have our hot chocolate first?" The boy asked, the allure of his mothers' hot cocoa too great to wait until she returned from her errand.

"Hmmm? Oh yes...yes, of course," Mrs. Wellings said distractedly. Mentally, she formulated a plan. She thanked the Lord for twenty-four-hour drug stores, especially when her husband owned said establishment. "Tell daddy I'll be right back, would you love?"

"Yes, Momma," Jesse said.

Balancing the two mugs of hot chocolate in one hand and grabbing a handful of Christmas tree cookies in the other, Jesse sought out his friend. He didn't care what Noel said, he knew she was hungry; she'd told him before her family almost never had food at home.

CHAPTER THREE

Jana glanced around the carefully decorated room. Crimson poinsettias and deep green holly decorated the table. Each place setting held a brilliant white plate trimmed in silver with a precisely folded green napkin shaped like a swan. The crystal goblets were a bit over the top; but they brought everything nicely together especially when the Christmas candles were lit casting a warm glow over the table.

The food, made with love, was a feast to behold, and she hoped that her family would love every single detail. She sighed, *who was she kidding?* John and the kids would have no idea how much prep work was involved, but she wanted it to be perfect just the same.

"Jesse...Noel! Dinner's ready!" Mrs. Wellings called for the two children.

Noel hopped to her feet, "Let's go! I'm starving!"

"Ah man, I was almost finished." Jesse stepped back admiring his work. He'd enjoyed drawing her. She made it easy cracking jokes and telling funny stories. He didn't understand how she could be so funny living in the home she lived in.

"We'll finish later. Come on my stomach's eating on my backbone." Noel's raspy voice joked.

Jesse chuckled, then stopped. Noel used that punchline often, but was she literally starving? He had no idea what that felt like. Did his friend suffer when she wasn't at his house? One look at her thin frame and hollowed cheeks told him all he needed to know.

"Yeah let's go. I bet I can beat ya!" Jesse jeered. Streaking past Noel, he dropped his sketch pad on the floor.

Noel almost took the bait and followed, but her eyes fell upon the picture Jesse had drawn. It was incredible; no it was better than incredible. Noel had no idea Jesse was so talented. The charcoal drawn picture had caught every minute detail about her, and yet changed a great many things as well. Jesse's artistic skills far surpassed that of a child of nine years. *Was he a prodigy?* She thought proud she remembered the big word she was taught in reading class.

In the portrait, her dirty stringy hair was soft, wavy, and flowed down her thin shoulders. Her clothes were clean, free of holes, and her face glowed with happiness. She looked as if she'd lived a lifetime filled with healthy family meals and always had clean, warm clothes on her back.

Noel smiled, one day she'd really be like that. Happy, loved, cared for...one day–

"Hey what are you doing?" Jesse asked breaking through her thoughts, coming back into the room. He cocked his head to the side studying Noel's expression.

"The picture," Noel said.

Jesse wrinkled his face, scrutinizing his work. "Well, it needs some work, but it–" Jesse's words stopped in his throat as Noel ran to his side and wrapped him in a tight embrace.

"Jesse Wellings, you're gonna be a famous artist someday." With her eyes clenched tight, she tried to prevent the tears of pride from leaving her eyes. She loved her friend, in her eyes he was perfect.

"Yeah right, I'm gonna be a skinned artist if we let dinner grow cold. Come on!" Jesse wriggled out of her grasp. Grabbing her hand, Jesse pulled Noel down the hall before his Momma started counting.

CHAPTER FOUR

Noel ate until her jaws grew sore. Her belly stuck out a good three inches over her already snug jeans. A large roasted chicken, buttery mashed potatoes, flaky, light rolls, five different veggies, and a table loaded down with made-from-scratch desserts completed her holiday meal. Jana Wellings was the queen of creating belly-busting Southern cuisine.

If it weren't for the Wellings, she would've eaten a tiny can of beanie weenies she had saved from the evening before and went to bed ready to sleep her winter break away. Most of her peers hated school, but she couldn't wait to get back. At school she was well-fed, loved by her teachers, and the best part was she got to spend six blissful hours a day in peace—away from her parents.

"Oh, you know what?" Mr. Wellings said. His voice rang overly loud to the room at large.

"What dear?" Mrs. Wellings asked enthusiastically with a twinkle in her eye, she too spoke way louder than necessary.

"I forgot to call Pastor Williams and wish his family a Merry Christmas! Would you all please excuse me for a moment?" Mr. Wellings wiped his mouth with the green napkin that had once been a swan and excused himself from the meal. On his way out of the room he bent over to kiss his wife. "Thank you dear, dinner was delicious."

She looked up at her husband and beamed. "Hurry back dear," Mrs. Wellings said barely able to conceal her glee.

Jesse and Noel shared a look with each other that asked, *have they lost their minds?* Seconds later however, they'd forgotten the adult's odd behavior and sat in agony as their bellies were ready to burst from the obscene amount of food they'd consumed.

"Alright then, can I interest you kids in some more hot chocolate?" Mrs. Wellings asked, seeing the children had cleared their plates.

Simultaneously Jesse groaned 'no,' and Noel shouted 'yes!' Jana chuckled at the pair, she stood and began to gather the dirty dishes.

Suddenly, a *bang* sounded from the roof and the jingle of sleigh bells filled Noels ears. Her head snapped to attention, the food stupor that had cast its spell on her forgotten. Could it be, had he not forgotten her after all? There was talk at school that he didn't really exist. Noel pushed her chair back and looked to Mrs. Wellings.

"WHAT. IS. THAT?" Noel shouted, her eyes growing the size of saucers.

"Oh dear, I don't know," Jana's eyes filled with tears at the wonder lighting up the young child's face. "Hurry, let's put our shoes and coats on then go see, shall we?" The tears threatened to spill from Jana's eyes as she witnessed the joy of a child in its purest form.

Jesse had already bolted from the room. He could be heard stumbling back up the hallway. Noel laughed when he reappeared with an arm full of shoes, socks, and mittens. His jacket hung loosely from one side of his body.

"Here," he thrust Noel's shoes under her nose. She snatched them from his hands and crammed her sockless feet into the hole-ridden sneakers.

"Come on," Noel cried dashing to the front door the sole of her right shoe flapping with each step.

Jesse followed, still wriggling into his coat while trying to stuff his hands into the thick blue wool mittens Santa left in his stocking.

It was a beautiful evening, the moon shone brightly on the snow-covered ground glittering like tiny diamonds across the land. Noel smiled at the sight. In her trailer park, nothing looked that beautiful.

She stood in the front yard, her dainty neck bent backwards, intently staring at the roof of the house. "Look," she pointed her bare arm into the air.

Her breath came out in fluffy puffs. She shivered from the cold. Jesse looked down at the warm coat hugging his body. Silently he slid the coat from his shoulders and slipped it around Noel.

Growing impatient, the excited girl grabbed Jesse's head. Physically, she turned his head from her to the sleigh tracks that adorned the Wellings snowcapped roof.

"Is he...is Santa here?" Noel's eyes shone with fresh tears.

Mrs. Wellings voice rang from the back yard. "Hurry guys, back here!"

In a dash, like little rabbits, the two babes ran to the backyard, snow flying behind them in clouds of sparkling dust.

"What is it?" They shouted, their eyes roaming every bit of the yard and roof hoping for a glimpse of Ol' St. Nick.

Something shiny caught Noel's eye on the ground. She missed the size six women's foot prints next to the glittery trail; she also missed the two by four that created Santa's sleigh marks propped against the house.

Instead, she asked pointing at the ground. "What's that?" A trail of confetti snowflakes and glitter leading to the back door of the Wellings home caught her eye.

"Is he–there?" The child stammered, excitement robbing her of the ability to speak coherently.

Mrs. Wellings laughed at the child's excitement. "Why don't you go inside and see?"

With a squeal once again, the two children dashed into the home, and followed the trail of sparkling snowflakes. The trail wound down the hall, through the sitting room, and continued into the family room.

Mr. Wellings stood in front of the fireplace looking down at two ashy boot prints that could be none other than Santa's. Noel's eyes roamed the room and fell upon the Christmas tree.

She loved the Wellings' Christmas tree. The fresh pine tree was filled with a great many homemade ornaments. Several of the precious mementos she had made over the last few years and gifted to the Wellings family as a Christmas gift. However, this time it wasn't the ornaments that caught her eye, but the tiny pile of brightly wrapped gifts that stood out. They hadn't been there before dinner.

Frozen, her eyes grew wide and she dared not move. Could maybe one of those gifts be for her? Had she not been forgotten after all?

Mrs. Wellings came up behind her lightly patting the girl's shoulder,

"Those are for you dear."

"All of them? What about Jesse?" She asked worried about her friend.

"Well there might be a little something for Jesse under the tree as well, but Santa visited him this morning."

Mrs. Wellings laughed as her words fell on deaf ears. Both children dove head first into the tiny pile of gifts.

"Oh wow!" Noel exclaimed as she slipped a new fleece lined sweater over her head. "It feels so fuzzy," she giggled. The soft material felt wonderful against her skin.

She continued ripping brightly wrapped snowman covered paper from her gifts. Each drug store bought toy was better than the last in Noel's eye. Mrs. Wellings breathed a sigh of relief knowing the gifts would bring the child a tiny glimmer of happiness during the season of Hope.

She wished she'd been more prepared, but who'd have thought such a bright, sweet, thoughtful child would come from the twisted, sick home the Miracles provided. How they could completely forget Christmas was unfathomable.

It wasn't the lack of gifts that set Jana on edge. She knew gifts were nice, and not all families were as fortunate as hers, but was it too much to ask to give up the bottle for one day to celebrate the holiday with their child. Even if they weren't believers of what Christmas stood for, couldn't they have taken the afternoon off to just love on the child they brought into this world?

Sighing, Jana reminded herself some people were a victim of their own addictions. She was blessed beyond all measure to have Noel as an extension of their family. The Miracle's loss was her gain.

"This is the best birthday ever!" Noel sung as she coated her lips in the new princess Chapstick Santa gifted her.

"I didn't know it was your birthday!" Jesse said jumping to his feet. The boy's face dropped in despair; how had he not known her birthday? Was he the worst friend ever?

"That's why my Momma named me Noel." The beautiful girl turned her face up to her friend.

"Wait right here," Jesse grabbed his sketch pad and took off. Noel shook her head but went back to playing with her new baby doll and stroller.

Fifteen minutes later, Jesse returned with a white unwrapped gift box.

"Happy birthday Noel," he handed her the gift.

"What's in it?" She asked. Raising her eyebrows, she shook what felt like an empty box. "You pulling a prank on me?" She squinted her eyes at Jesse trying to determine if her friend was messing with her.

"Just open it," Jesse said impatiently, his normally pale cheeks growing a bright pink. Why Noel made him blush was beyond him. He was fine any other time.

Gently Noel peeled back the lid of the box. Inside was the picture Jesse had drawn. He added a window pane behind Noel and deep into the background you could see a reindeer driven sleigh being pulled through the starry night sky.

Noel sat looking at the picture saying nothing. "If you don't like it I can fix it," Jesse held his hand out nervously to take the drawing back.

"Don't you dare take it from me Jesse Wellings, I love it!" Noel hugged the drawing to her chest. Jesse winced as she crinkled the paper in her embrace. He was glad she liked it, that portrait was the best work he'd ever done.

Jana watched the exchange, her heart overflowing with love and pride in how talented her son was. She had never seen such work from him or any other child of his age. "I hate to break up the party here, but Noel, it's getting late sweetie. You may need to head home, I'm sure your parents will worry if you're not back soon."

The light fled Noel's eyes, but she got up and picked up her new toys. "Yes, ma'am."

"Pack your gifts up, and I'll make you a plate of goodies to take home." Jesse had shared with his mother many times of how Noel's family didn't have enough food most of the time. The only blessing that Jana could see in the Miracle's home was they were smart enough to only have one child.

"Thank you," Noel said hoping Mrs. Wellings packed enough food to last until school started back.

CHAPTER FIVE

"Mom, can't I just walk Noel home," Jesse pleaded. He wanted a few minutes alone with her before she went back to the horror that was her life.

"No love, it's dark, cold, and Noel has several packages to carry, but if you get your hat and gloves you can ride with us." Jana said leaving no room for discussion.

"Okay," Jesse groaned wanting time away from his mom to make sure Noel would be okay once she got back home.

Jesse need not worry; his mother had the same intention. "Noel, will you...will you be okay dear?" Mrs. Wellings asked.

"Yeeessss," Noel answered not quite sure what she was being asked.

Mrs. Wellings gripped the steering wheel tightly and tried again, "Honey are you safe? Is there anything you need at home?"

She got it, her home was different than Jesse's. They wanted to know what happened behind closed doors. She'd never tell—her Momma threatened that she'd be taken away if she ever told anyone. "Yes...I mean no. I mean, I'm fine thank you."

Fine was an overstatement however, as the Wellings family car pulled into the Miracle drive. Noel sensed she was in for a long night.

The fighting still raged on from earlier that day, only this time there was begging and pleading for her father not to leave. Mrs. Miracle even promised to quit drinking. Noel knew it was a lie, but those magic words kept her father around, most of the time.

"Oh dear," Mrs. Wellings distress grew.

"It's okay, they'll fall asleep soon. They always do." Noel assured the woman.

"Can we help you carry your things in?" Mrs. Wellings asked her eyes set in hard concentration.

"No, it's better if I do it," Noel answered.

"We understand," Mrs. Wellings smiled sadly in the rearview mirror. A wave of angry passion raged in her chest. How could she help the child without her being forced into the state system?

"When I grow up, I won't be like them. I want to be like you." The sweet child leaned over the seat, wrapped her arms around Mrs. Wellings neck, and planted a sweet kiss on the woman cheek.

Noel thought she smelled nice like expensive soap and vanilla. Her own mother reeked of sweat, cheap whiskey, and stale cigarette smoke.

As Noel climbed out of the Wellings' sedan loaded down with bags of food, toys, and new clothes, she felt something she had never felt in her entire life–loved.

CHAPTER SIX

Fifteen Years Later

Christmas break was upon her, and Noel wondered what she should do. There was no one to celebrate with. A trip away would be nice, but where? Looking at her bank account, she could see there was no money for anything extravagant. However, she needed to get away. It had been a rough year since she had broken things off with Alec. He was too much like her father to live with.

She'd sworn men off for good. No matter what she did, she attracted the wrong type of men. Drunks who wanted to live off her little income without contributing to the bills. She was done. She had her kids at school and that was enough for her, for now.

Her cell phone buzzed, vibrating against her kitchen table. "Hello," Noel answered her phone cautiously. She knew the area code but very few people knew how to reach her from there.

"Noel Miracle?" A young female voice asked curtly.

"This is Noel." She answered guardedly.

"Noel, this is Sara Rhymes, Jesse Wellings' assistant. I've been asked to call and deliver some unfortunate news."

"Okay," Noel's throaty voice drawled.

"Mr. Wellings wanted me to let you know his mother Mrs. Wellings has suffered a massive heart attack. She…" Here the assistant hesitated. Noel could tell she'd rather be doing anything else than delivering this news. Noel's heart pounded, the woman's next words could break her heart. "She's asking to see you Ms. Miracle."

"Jana? She's alive?" Noel asked praying her lungs would relax enough to take in a deep breath.

"The doctors are unsure of her prognosis, but yes she's alive. Jana needs surgery but right now she's too weak to survive it. They have sent her home, but she's in a very fragile and weakened state. You may want to prepare yourself to say goodbye."

Terror thronged her body–*goodbye?* "I'll be there by tomorrow night." Noel's voice quivered.

"Great, I'll make arrangements for your stay." Sara Rhymes answered briskly.

"Oh no, I can get a hotel...or..."

"Mrs. Wellings wishes are for you to stay in the Wellings' home. Is that acceptable?" The young woman sounded as if Noel was making her life difficult.

"Oh, yes...sure that's...okay." Noel gave in, she'd hate to upset Jana by refusing.

"I'll let Jess-" an uncomfortable giggle. "I mean, Mr. Wellings know you'll be there tomorrow evening, say around dinner time?"

"Yes, that'll work thank you Ms. Rhymes." Noel answered.

"Good evening," the young woman said before the line went dead.

Noel sank into her second-hand couch broken hearted. What would the world be like without Jana Wellings? She should've gone to see her before now, regret settled in the pit of her stomach.

"Oh Jana, please forgive me," she whispered before calling her employer about a leave of absence.

CHAPTER SEVEN

Noel breathed in deeply, the sweet Kentucky air filling her nose. There really was no place like home. Aside from the new fuel station she had stopped at to fuel up, the small town appeared virtually untouched by time.

Just a few blocks away she could see the town square. Right in the center of the square a large wishing well once sat. She smiled thinking of all the pennies she'd tossed in the well. It had long since been filled in with dirt and used as a raised flower bed, but she could still see the fountain shooting water in the air in her mind. She could feel the tiny droplets rain down on her little hand as she contemplated what her wish would be. It was always the same–that God would deliver her from her parents.

Now the old fountain held a huge Christmas tree surrounded by tons of crimson and white poinsettias. The tree looked as if it were being decked out with tons of lights and brightly colored baubles. A team of city workers were stringing evergreen garland and lights all over the little town. Noel made a mental note to swing back by in a few days to see the final result.

"Am I dreaming or is that Noel Miracle I see?" The peppy southern twang could belong to none other than Cassandra Reynolds. Noel winced but turned towards the all too familiar voice.

"Cassandra," Noel plastered a fake smile across her face.

"What are you doing in these parts? Your ma and pa have been gone for ages." Cassandra hadn't changed much. Her curves were curvier, and her long red locks flowed down her back in perfect spirals; but those attributes just made her even more beautiful.

"Oh, uh Jana–" Noel began.

"Of course, you came to spend some time with Jana." Cassandra placed a hand over her heart. "I'm so glad, she's missed you something terrible. Every time I see her she talks of you," Cassandra didn't pause to take a breath.

"How is...he...Jesse?" Noel asked.

"You still not talking to that boy? Mmm, girl!" Cassandra shook her head as if she hadn't played her part. "Broke his little ol' heart didn't ya? Noel, you sure have a stubborn streak. Now don't get upset by me saying so, but you messed up big time with that boy. He loved you dearly. Why just the other day I was saying to Jemma Jones..."

"Cassandra, I have to go," Noel said sliding behind the wheel of her car.

"Don't be a stranger you hear!" Cassandra waved her perfectly manicured fingers in little ripples through the air.

"I won't," Noel said through tightly clenched teeth.

Fire engine red climbed up Noel's face as she thought of the day Jesse broke her heart. Cassandra could play cute and coy, but she knew what she was doing that day and there was no undoing it. Cassandra played a huge part in the break of Jesse and Noel's friendship, and Noel had no use for the girl. But, if she learned anything from Jana Wellings, it was always to be a lady.

Throwing her beat-up 87' Ford Mustang GT in reverse, she took off, leaving Cassandra staring open mouthed in a cloud of dust. So much for being a lady.

CHAPTER EIGHT

She pulled into the long drive that led to the Wellings home. The quaint brownstone was as it always had been–beautiful, perfect and filled with an unmeasurable amount of love. Noel had spent many days and evenings in that home with the Wellings family.

Jana Wellings made sure Noel had a hot meal every night and warm clothing on her back; especially when her parents drank too much. Their drinking was out of hand more often than not.

The home was all too familiar but the feeling of dread upon entering it was new to Noel. Until she and Jess had their falling out, she'd loved the place and considered it an extension of her own home. She had spent countless summer hours romping in the yard, climbing trees, and drinking homemade lemonade while concocting hers and Jesse's next adventure.

Now the place she once loved was tainted with pain from the past. Her guilt of letting anger get the best of her caused a lump of regret to make home in her gut. Why did teenage foolishness still hurt as an adult?

"Get over it Noel...it's time," Noel whispered to herself. The rumble of the Mustangs engine cut off with the turn of a key, but Noel made no attempt to move.

What if Jesse was in there? What would he say to her? Worse yet, what would she say to him?

A knock at her window caused her to jump and cry out. Her heart raced, and she fumbled for her keys ready to bolt.

"Noel?" A man's voice asked.

Turning to look at the tall figure standing next to her car, Noel's heart jumped to her throat. All she could see was his pants. She sat too low to the ground to see his face. Was it Jesse? Please God, not yet. I'm not ready to see him.

"Noel, is that you?" The jolly voice of Mr. Wellings boomed from outside her vehicle. He bent over to show his face.

"Oh, thank God," she breathed, heavily slumping into her seat. She needed more time before seeing Jesse.

Putting on her brightest smile, Noel looked up to Mr. Wellings. She yanked on the handle of the car door swinging it open.

Strong arms wrapped around her body pinning her arms to her side. "Oh, it's so good to see you! Where have you been? It's been what...five years?"

Six. It'd been six years since her mom called her home last. She'd been arrested on drug charges and needed to be bailed out. Noel came home, bailed her mother out, then let the woman who birthed her know she was done. No more bailing out of jail, no more cleaning up messes that her boyfriend of the week caused, no more disappointments waiting for her mom to act like anything more than the person who carried her in her belly for nine months.

After that day Noel changed her number, cutting the woman from her life. There was nothing left for her. Many years prior, her dad finally had enough of his wife and fled—never to be heard from again. No goodbye to his wife or daughter, he just disappeared.

John and Jana Wellings were the only people she missed now. They truly were her family. The kind couple had taken Noel under their wings and treated her just as they would've their own. When she left, however, she all but cut them from her life as well.

"It's so good to see you Pops," Noel said into the old man's neck. Tears leaked from her eyes as she clung to the man who was the only real father figure she'd ever known.

"Oh, our girl!" He cried, tears leaked from the old man's eyes as well. "Jana's going to be so happy to see you. She's missed you something fierce," he said drawing back, but keeping his hands on her shoulders. "She won't like how thin you've gotten that's for sure."

Noel groaned, "I eat just fine, Pops."

"Yeah, yeah," Mr. Wellings walked her to the door his arm still around her shoulder. "Come on in, you have to see the new television. Jesse got it for us a few weeks back. It's a little too nice. I haven't quite figured out how to use the remote, yet."

Noel closed her eyes trying not to flinch at the sound of her old friend's name. She had to let it go. They were all different people now...it was over.

"Is he...here?" Noel asked peering at the home.

"Oh no. Here give me your bag. No Jesse's working right now. He opened that new art studio. I'm sure he told you all about it, huh?" Mr. Wellings stuck his chest out proud of his son's accomplishment. Noel smiled, glad he accepted his son's passion. At one point, he pushed Jesse to become a pharmacist like himself.

"I, uh...," Noel started. Stepping over the threshold of the home, instantly a rush of memories and emotions washed over her.

"John, is that my Noel? Send her back right away!" Jana's voice traveled from somewhere in the back of the house.

Mr. Wellings chuckled, "She's sick as they come but still manages to push me around. Come, you can visit with her, and I'll put your bags in your old room. If that's okay?"

"I'd love that," Noel's throaty voice grew deeper at the thought of using her old room.

She wondered if the Wellings had changed it at all. Her room at the Wellings was a paradise compared to her real home. It was a haven when her parents drank too much and tore the house apart. Or later when her dad moved away, and her mother decided to throw all-nighters with the town's rowdy crowd.

"Go on in, hon. She can't get out of bed much right now." Mr. Wellings said.

Walking to the master bedroom, she rose her hand to knock, but the door was partially open. "Come in my dear, don't fool with good manners. I'm dying to see you child!"

Pushing the double door to the master suite open, Noel stepped inside the dark room. "Switch on that little lamp there, dear," Jana pointed to a lamp on her bedside table."

Obediently, Noel did as directed, but immediately she wished she hadn't. One look at Jana Wellings, and it was clear to see just how sick she was. The once plump woman had lost weight, and her color was a terrible shade of gray. Her once youthful face was wrinkled, and her eyes drooped in exhaustion.

"Oh, you can just get over the nonsense that's running through your head right now. No number of tears will change what's happened. I made my peace with my Maker, and I'm ready to go home if He calls me. There's just one loose end I need to wrap up before that day."

"Oh?" Noel asked. She wanted to say more but her words became choked by the sob that worked its way up her throat.

Covering her mouth to stifle her sobs, Noel stood in the dark room facing the woman who was like a mother to her. The woman she abandoned because of her selfish pride.

"Oh my! Come here, my child." Jana flung her arms open ready to embrace the girl she'd missed dearly.

Noel sat on the side of the women's bed crumpling into her thin arms. "I'm okay, my girl. Seeing you has already brought me a world of joy in just a matter of seconds. Don't cry my love, we don't blame you for leaving this town. We just missed you is all."

"I'm so sorry...so sorry. I should've called, but I needed–"

"You needed a clean start is what you needed. Believe me, I understood that. We all did, even Jesse eventually..." Jana's words trailed off.

Noel sat up. "I let too much time go by, now I'm afraid–"

"That there isn't much left?" Jana asked.

Noel shook her head then slowly nodded. "I suppose." She looked down at Jana's frail bruised hand. It must have been from an I.V. in the hospital.

"Honey, none of us is guaranteed tomorrow. At least with me, I can prepare, make amends with those that need it, and love those who are in my life a little harder. And if I get more time than anticipated, I get the blessing of an extended life. After my little scare, any time I have left I plan to take full advantage of."

"You've always been so strong." Noel sniffled.

Mrs. Wellings smiled at the young woman who was still a child to her. "Maybe I learned that from you."

Noel shook her head. She wasn't strong. She ran when things got hard, always. She ran to the Wellings when life got tough at home, she ran 300 miles away when Jesse broke her heart, and she ran when her mom's ridiculous schemes became too much to bear. She was a runner, nothing strong about that she thought.

"Can I get you anything?" Noel asked wanting to protect and care for the sweet woman.

"No dear, John's an excellent nurse and cares for me rather well. I do need to nap, I'm afraid. I took some pain medicine just before you arrived. Why don't you go unpack, and get settled back in? John will order in dinner. He never learned to cook well you know, and our housekeeper is off today."

"That sounds wonderful...thank you for having me here." Noel said shyly.

"No love, thank you for coming back home. You're one of us you know." Jana gave the girl another quick squeeze before snuggling into her down comforter and shutting her eyes. The thought of leaving this world was a little less daunting now that she had her entire family close by.

CHAPTER NINE

Sara Rhymes, assistant director at Wellings Art Gallery, found Jesse in his office. He had his back to her and was staring out the window at the town below. Wistfully, Sara watched him, knowing he agonized over his mother, and now the arrival of Noel Miracle.

Noel, the girl who left a gaping hole in the heart of Jesse Wellings. A hole Sara desperately tried to fill, unsuccessfully she might add.

"Your father called...She's arrived. I made plans for us to join them for dinner tonight," Sara said calmly in her businesslike persona she kept while they were at work. Inside, she was dying to please the man she'd given her heart to.

"It's nice, isn't it?" He asked not turning around.

Leaning her head to the side, confused she asked, "What is nice?"

"The town, the decorations are almost up for the tree lighting ceremony. It was my favorite thing to do at Christmas time. Me, my family, and..." He didn't say Noel's name. He knew it would upset Sara if he did. She was jealous, but she needn't be. He had long since removed Noel Miracle from his heart. She was nothing more than a childhood memory.

Sara smiled puzzled, "Yeah? What's got you so sentimental today?"

Jesse let out a sigh, "I don't know. Just thinking of when I was a kid. It was nice not having to be such an...adult I guess."

Sara giggled, "Well, Mr. Wellings, I for one am glad you're all grown up. Who would I marry otherwise?"

They weren't engaged officially, but they both knew it was a matter of time. She had it all planned out. A spring wedding, Jamaican cruise, and a wildly successful life. Just she and her husband. Sara had no desire to have children; they'd just get in the way of her plans to take Jesse and his work global. He had the talent, and she had the drive.

Jesse turned and smiled gratefully at Sara. "I'll be down soon. We can stop by the pharmacy on our way to mom's for some fresh flowers."

"Okay, I'll start closing up. Yarma Zans from New York called again. They need final approval for the pieces you plan to show in the spring gala." Sara switched gears wanting to drive thoughts of his past – of the girl who once held his heart – far from his mind.

"Okay, I'll let you know tomorrow..." Jesse turned his back to her again.

He smiled, thinking of years past when he and Noel would run around the square filling up on hot chocolate and his mother's famous cookies during the Tree Lighting Festival. His mom would bake for days to have enough cookies for the celebration. He and Noel always kept close to Jana in the days leading up to the festival in hopes of taste testing the cookies as they were pulled fresh from the oven. When Noel was around, his mother would give in and give them a plated filled with cookies and a large glass of cold milk. If they were lucky, she'd make hot cocoa for them.

He sighed, things had changed drastically since she left. His heart pounded with fear as he wondered how she'd receive him. How would he react when he saw her?

Would she look at him as she did that day? With pain beyond what he could have imagined, or will she have forgiven him? Surely, after all these years his past transgressions would not sting so bad.

Could he win back the affection of his best friend after all these years, or would she make him suffer forever?

CHAPTER TEN

Jana had said Noel was one of them–a Wellings? Noel knew the Wellings loved her and she them, but was she really one of them? Jesse made sure she knew different when they were teens.

Based on the conversations she had with the Wellings, Jesse hadn't shared with them why she stopped coming around. They just assumed she needed a clean break from her parents. And then of course, she started her career and that demanded much of her time.

Even during summer and winter breaks, she spent much of her free time planning for her students. Of course, Alec had been a factor taking much of her time as well, but he was in the past now. She made a clean break with him, and not a moment too soon, it sounded like. She read in the paper he had been arrested on drunk driving charges and was caught with a girl under the age of eighteen. He was the epitome of a creep.

Just get over it, surely Jesse has by now, she thought to herself refolding her clothing before putting them away into the dresser. The Wellings had bought the dresser when she was a little girl. Smiling, she was glad to see they didn't change her room at all. John shared with her he hoped one day they'd have a granddaughter who'd love the room as she had.

A knock at the door broke through her thoughts. "Noel?" Mr. Wellings voice called to her.

"Come in," she answered.

"Good, you're getting settled in, I see. Is everything okay? I know the bed may seem smaller than it did when you were younger."

"Oh no, the room's perfect. It's nice being back." She smiled warmly at him. Compared to her one-bedroom apartment, the Wellings' home was a palace.

"It's nice having you here. Listen, I'm running to town real fast. Can you keep an ear out for Jana? I expect she'll sleep until I get back, but just in case."

"Of course! It'd be my pleasure." She answered.

"I'm picking up Mexican food this evening, Jana said you always loved Garcia's, and she does as well." Her mouth watered at the thought.

"You have no idea how amazing that sounds. If I can't have home cooking made by Momma Jay's sweet hands, then Garcia's is second best. But don't go out of your way for me—just whatever is fine."

Mr. Wellings turned to leave, "No trouble at all. Jesse's coming and bringing his new girlfriend. I know you two can't wait to see each other."

Noel's face paled. "Oh great," she said, gulping loudly. Mr. Wellings didn't hear the dread that filled her voice as he whistled a catchy show tune she couldn't quite make out.

*   *   *

"It's so good to have you all under the same roof again," Jana's normally strong voice distorted by weakness. The heart disease had stolen much of her gusto.

Noel turned her eyes from the woman she loved like a mother. Jana had once been a healthy, vibrant woman as jolly as her husband. Now she could hardly walk without assistance.

The sweet woman wrapped an arm around Noel's shoulders and squeezed. Warm hugs. Jana always gave big warm hugs that made Noel feel safe from the troubles the world freely gifted her. Warm hugs that smelled of vanilla and love. Hugs she had missed more than she wanted to admit.

"How long has it been?" Sara Rhymes, Jesse's secretary/girlfriend, asked with a plastic smile plastered across her beautiful face. Noel took an instant dislike to the girl, and she felt the beautiful young lady felt the same about her.

"Six years now, isn't it dear?" Jana looked at Noel whose eyes stayed

27

trained on her plate wondering why she wanted to claw out Sara Rhymes' eyes every time she touched Jesse.

"Yes," her voice just above a whisper. Pushing her food around on her plate she tried not to watch as Sara pawed at Jesse.

"Well, I think it's real nice that the Wellings took you in like they did. Why, stories of what Jesse sacrificed for you is what attracted me to him in the first place!" Sara gushed.

"What Jesse did for me?" Noel's voice asked hollowly. *You crafty vixen,* Noel thought, *you're going to hit where it hurts right out the gate.*

Meeting Jesse's eyes for the first time since he had arrived for dinner, Noel's heart jumped to her throat. She opened her mouth to ask Jesse what exactly had he sacrificed for her. "Noel, I..." he shook his head, then looked to his mother for help.

Jana grabbed Noel's wrist hoping to silence the girl. "Oh John! I just remembered Mary Straus brought over her famous apple cinnamon cake! It's right on the counter there in the kitchen. Could you be a dear...?"

"No," Noel shouted, so startled by her own outbursts she tried again. "No, I'll get it Mr. Wellings. I'll be right back." Gently pulling away from Jana's grip she leapt halfway to the kitchen door, her dinner plate still clutched in her hands.

Must he be so amazing looking? Like could he have gotten fat, adult acne, or something? She thought as she slammed down the dessert plates. *And does his girlfriend have to be so stinking perfect? Couldn't she at least get some lettuce stuck in her pearly whites? Like really, the woman was flawless from her tiny heart shaped face to her itty bitty, perfectly manicured feet.*

Opening and closing each drawer with more force than necessary, she looked for the silverware drawer.

"Need some help?" Darn, even his velvety smooth voice made her heart ache.

"No, I'm fine...you can just..." *You can just move out of my way bucko.*

"Noel." He was too close. Grabbing her upper arms, he turned her to face him. Turning her large eyes to his, she waited.

He cleared his throat, "Are we...are we okay?"

Probably not, she thought. "What? Oh, you mean that stuff in high school? I'm over it. I just...it feels weird being back is all..."

Jesse hesitated, "So you're not upset with me?"

More than you know buddy. "No," her voice raising twelve octaves. "I barely remember what caused us to—our friendship to...um..."

"Break," he said softly, taking another step closer. Alarms rang in her mind, it was becoming hard to breathe.

"Yes," the word fell from her lips. "Break..."

"I–" his words caught in his throat.

"Jess, Noel? Did you two need help?" Mr. Wellings asked entering the room, his hands laden with dirty dinner dishes.

"Oh no, Pops, let me get those!" Noel took the plates from the old man's hands. "Jesse was just showing me where the serving knife was. We're coming now."

"Well...alright," he said looking from Noel to Jesse. "You okay, Noel? Your face looks mighty red."

"Yes, I'm fine. Just a bit warm in here. Could you gentleman take care of dessert for me, please? I have to make an important phone call." Noel pushed the dishes into Jesse's hands.

"Of course, dear. Shall we wait for you?" Mr. Wellings asked picking up the cake.

"No, please don't. I believe I'll turn in for the night after my call. It will take a while—work stuff," she answered.

"Well, good night then," Mr. Wellings said.

"Noel, maybe we can spend some time together this week. Come see the gallery. I'd love to know what you think." Jesse offered.

"Sure," she answered with a slight shrug of her shoulders, hating the fact that she did want to see his gallery, very much. "Please excuse me."

CHAPTER ELEVEN

Summer 2001

A lazy, hot, summer day had sapped the two children of their strength. Going inside would be to admit defeat for the day, and that just wasn't done on summer break. Instead, they found comfort in the shade of an enormous, ancient, oak tree on the outer edge of the Wellings' property. Lazily, they slurped down Popsicles that melted down their arms quicker than they could eat them, dying their skin shades of purple, blue, and red.

"When we grow up, I'm going to take care of you forever," Jesse said in a fierce whisper.

Noel's already large eyes grew bigger. "You will?"

"Yeah, and if your parents try to come take you away, I'll fight em," he said clenching sticky hands into tight fists.

"Why don't they love me like your mom and dad love you?" Noel asked. She wasn't sad just matter of fact.

"Because they're dumb, and dumb people don't deserve people like you." Jesse whispered the word dumb, to him it was as near a cuss as anything. Noel's tiny heart filled with so much love she wondered how much more she could take.

"Jesse?" She asked wrinkling her brow.

"Yeah?" he asked, licking blue slush off his arm.

"Do you believe in God?" She asked looking intently at her friend, her protector.

"I do, don't you?" he asked shocked by her question.

"I wasn't sure at first, but I prayed for a new family, and he gave me you." Noel leaned her head onto Jesse's shoulder. He smelled of sunshine and sweaty boy. *I love you, Jesse Wellings*, she thought in her mind as she closed her eyes, enjoying the peace that came with being close to him.

Noel woke with a start. She had dreamed of that sweet moment between she and Jesse many times. They were just kids, but she thought he'd always be her protector. She had been wrong. Maybe it had been wrong of her to place so much pressure on him. Had it been difficult for him to always watch her back? Had she been a burden he couldn't shake? They were both kids after all. She had just held him to a higher standard than the rest of the world.

It was early still but she was determined that while she stayed in the Wellings' home, she'd care for them as they had done for her many years ago. After a quick shower and a fresh change of clothing, she went to the kitchen to make breakfast.

However, there was already someone there. A young woman, cooking up a storm. "Good morning. Miss Noel, I believe?" She had a bit of an Irish accent that went along well with her red hair, short stature, and stocky frame.

"Yes, hello," Noel smiled at the portly woman. "Who are you?"

"I am Marta. I work for the Wellings family. I do the cooking and cleaning mostly. I wasn't here yesterday because it was my day off, but I'm here most every day except Mondays. On Mondays, Mr. Jesse comes for dinner, and they have take out. He used to take his Momma and Poppa out to eat, but Mrs. W stays inside most of the time now. I hate what's happening to her," the young woman eyes filled with sorrow and tears for just a moment before snapping back into the jovial chatterbox she undoubtedly was.

"Oh yes, I suppose if she weren't sick I'd have never met them to begin with. Mrs. W is the most excellent homemaker and, oh my, she cooks something fierce. Don't you agree?" Noel opened her mouth to answer but Marta plowed on.

"Oh, it's splendid to have another girl my age around. Don't get me wrong. I love, I mean I absolutely love, love, love Mr. and Mrs. W but it's nice to talk with people your own age, wouldn't you agree?" Marta expertly flipped bacon and scrambled eggs then flew to the other side of the room to start some toast.

"I…" Noel started.

"I like the looks of you–good sturdy gal. Your eyes are kind, not like that Sara Rhymes. Satan wrapped in pretty flesh if you ask me. Oh, I'd love to give her a whack! Oops, don't tell Mr. Jesse I said that. I don't want to hurt his feelings. If you don't mind me saying so, she is a piece of–"

"Marta! Breakfast smells wonderful as always," Mr. Wellings broke through the chatter.

"The very best of mornings to you, sir!" The young lady straightened her back and continued to work in hyperdrive. "Breakfast will be ready in a snap, don't you worry sir!"

"I never worry when you're here Marta." At his praise the young lady beamed. "Please excuse us for just a moment. I need to speak with Noel," Mr. Wellings gently guided Noel from the room. Once out of earshot of the exuberant housekeeper, Noel relaxed, allowing the breath she had been holding to escape.

"Don't go far. Breakfast is up in five minutes." Marta yelled after their retreating backs.

"Oh my," Noel said softly trying to catch her breath.

Chuckling Mr. Wellings turned to Noel. "I see you've met our Marta. She's something…but she does keep one from being lonely, and she's top notch at what she does."

"It certainly appears so." Then without warning Noel burst into a torrent of laughter. She laughed so long and so hard, she received a stitch in her side.

Soon, Mr. Wellings joined her. When the pair caught their breath, Mr. Wellings spoke, "I should've warned you."

Wiping tears from her eyes, "Not at all, it's okay I find her…refreshing actually."

"That she is! Listen, after breakfast do you mind running down to the pharmacy and grabbing Jana's medication? I called it in, and they know I'm sending you."

"Of course, anything else I can do while I'm out?" Noel asked ready to be of service in any way she could.

"No, that'll be it. I'd go myself, but Jana's having a bad morning," Mr. Wellings said his smile dropping.

"Can I do anything for her?" Still eager to please.

"No, after she eats and rests, I am sure she'd love a visit. Maybe you can read to her a bit over lunch." Noel smiled, she loved reading to Jana. She was the best kind of audience.

"That'd be wonderful," Noel smiled sadly.

"Alright you two, I've made enough bacon to choke a horse. Come and get it!" Marta popped around the corner, a tray laden with food resting on one arm while another tray loaded with steaming cups of coffee and all the fixings on the other.

CHAPTER TWELVE

"Dinner was certainly… interesting last night, wasn't it?" Sara asked, gripping Jesse's hand. She studied his face waiting for a reaction.

He pulled away, startled by her touch. "What…oh yes it was nice to have the family back together again."

"Family? Please, that freeloader could hardly be considered family!" Jesse's face wrinkled at her description of Noel. "Don't get me wrong, I don't blame her one bit…it's just, she's not family Jess. Should she be here? Now?" Sara's eyes bore into his.

Jesse felt anger stir in his heart at the words Sara spoke, but he answered with gentleness. "You don't have to be blood to be family. Mom wants her here."

"Well, whatever Jana wants—" Sara's voice dripped with jealousy. "But that girl doesn't belong in our world, with people like us." She pointed her cherry red nails at Jesse. *People like us?* He thought but let it go.

Sara had been raised a spoiled debutante, and Jesse, even though his parents were well off, was not raised to be spoiled. Not spoiled in a materialistic way that is; he was spoiled by love from his Momma, had a terrific relationship with his father, and he had Noel. Noel was his everything — when they were kids.

What was she now, just a memory? He had to remind himself that time had changed them all. Who knew what she was really like deep down. For all he knew, she could be just like her parents had been. He knew one thing however; she was more beautiful than she ever was during childhood, and when he got close to her, his heart pounded so hard he was afraid she could hear it.

He was going to have to keep a safe, friendly distance from Noel or he may lose all senses, then where would he be? If his father hadn't walked into the kitchen the other night, he may have done something very foolish indeed. Then where would they be?

CHAPTER THIRTEEN

The tinkle of the overhead bell made her smile. She missed that sound so much. Noel had gifted the bell to John Wellings years ago, after she received her first paycheck from a babysitting job. He always complained he couldn't hear when a customer walked through the front door. He was afraid some of the kids had been shoplifting when he was in the back filling prescriptions.

She had Mr. Owens from the hardware store help her install the little jingle bell. She never forgot the delight that small bell brought to Mr. Wellings. Noel didn't know if the bell kept teens from lifting candy and other goods, but it brought Pops a sense of security. His joy made her happy, and that was all that mattered in the end. She was delighted to know the new owner had kept the tiny memento.

As she glanced around the small shop, she felt a sense of relief. The new owner had kept the integrity of the store intact. When she heard Pops had retired, she was afraid his sweet shop would be ruined. As a teen, Noel herself worked there stocking shelves. There were even times where Mr. Wellings trusted her to deliver over the counter medications to those too sick to leave their homes.

"Miss, can I help you?" A boisterous voice boomed from above.

"Oh sorry, yes I'm here to pick up medication for Jana Wellings." Noel said glancing around the store she spent so many of her summers in, first as a child trailing Jesse then as a teen for summer work.

"Noel? Is that you, girl? Woo hoo, look at you!" The words flowed from a handsome lumberjack of a man who stood before her, a magnificent auburn beard covered most of his face.

"Jimmy? Jimmy Wren? Wow! I can't believe you're still here!" Noel shrieked.

"Yeah bought the place from the Wellings a few years back." Jimmy said proudly.

"You bought...oh you're the new Pharmacist? Good for you! I never would've thought..." she trailed off embarrassed about what she almost said.

His laugh was like thunder, "Don't be embarrassed. You and half the town knew me to be wild. But I met a girl, and she set me straight. She forced college on me where I got a fancy degree and came back home to marry her before some other man swooped her up."

"I'm so happy for you! Who's the lucky girl?" Noel asked, her eyes shone with happiness for her old friend.

Jimmy's eyes went dark. "Jennifer Lawler—you remember her, don't ya?" He asked.

"Real quiet, dark brown hair, tiny little thing?" Noel scrunched her eyes trying to remember the girl.

"That's her," his voice softened.

"Yes, we had some classes together senior year. How's she doing?" Noel smiled, glad Jimmy had found such a sweet girl. Back in high school, he was attracted to the wrong type of lady, and they always landed him in trouble. He had a soft spot for the ladies, especially the mean feisty ones.

The smile lines around his eyes faded, and his jaw set in a scowl, "Lost her in an accident a few years back."

"I'm so sorry," Noel's voice rasped, her hand flitted to her chest.

Jimmy cleared his throat, turning his back to her. "Let me grab that medication for you."

Noel hated to hear her old friend had suffered such a devastating loss, and she had no idea that it'd even happened. Time slips by so quickly, she thought, ashamed she hadn't called home more – that she hadn't kept in touch.

"Here you go. So how long are you in town?" Jimmy asked his smile firmly back in place.

"Um, well, I took off the last two weeks before winter break, and I plan to stay through the new year when school starts back, but it kind of depends on Jana's recovery."

"Yeah, it's a shame that is, there isn't a better woman in five counties than Jana Wellings." Jimmy smiled sadly. Noel loved his country twang.

"Agreed!" Noel gushed proud of the woman who raised her.

"How's Jesse? I haven't seen him in a while." Jimmy asked.

"I haven't seen him much yet, I met his um…" Noel grasped for a word to describe Jesse's significant other.

"His Sara?" Jimmy chuckled. "That girl's a piece of work, right there!"

"What makes you say…" the tinkle of the front door rang. An elderly couple walked in.

"Hello there, I'll be right with you!" Jimmy's loud, friendly voice called to them.

Turning back to Noel, he said, "Listen, let's have dinner and catch up before you go, I'd love to see what you've been up to since you escaped this place."

"Sure, I'd love that. It was good seeing you, Jim, you look great, really! See ya," Noel beamed at her old friend.

Walking back to her car, Noel smiled thinking of Jimmy Wren back in high school. He was wild, funny, and at times pure trouble. But he was good–natured, kind, and he was there for Noel when she and Jesse had their falling out.

"Wow, how lucky can I be to see you twice in one week!" Cassandra Reynolds drawled.

Crap! "Hey girl," Noel drawled back bearing her teeth. "Wish I could chat, but I have to get back to Jana." Noel held the prescription bag of medication in the air and shook it in Cassandra's face.

"Drat, well you can't avoid me forever sweetie." Cassandra sang.

Wanna bet? Noel thought.

"Ha-ha, sorry hon. I wish I had time to talk. Maybe next time?" Noel tried to look apologetic but was afraid she missed the mark.

"Uh huh, next time for sure! Bye, bye doll," Cassandra fanned her fingers in the air.

"Bye," Noel slid into her car and started the engine.

She just pulled out when a shout and a sharp rap on her window caused her to stomp on her break. "Noel wait!"

"For the love of…" *Jesse stinking Wellings*, she mouthed to herself.

Noel rolled her eyes putting her car into park. She should have known better, you can't go into a town the size of Old Harmony and not run into half the townsfolk.

Rolling her window down, she looked up to Jesse. *God he's handsome*, she thought. His lanky frame had filled out nicely. He also had an incredible sun kissed glow to his skin, considering it was the middle of winter.

He wore loose fitting jeans, a plain black tee, and a black leather jacket. She was used to seeing him in more formal attire, but she liked the casual look so much more. He had a day of growth on his face which added an element of raw, masculine maturity. Noel felt blood rush to her cheeks as she examined his lips.

"Hey," one side of his mouth turned up in a boyish grin.

"Hey, I was just picking up meds for Momma Jay." Noel said, trying not to drool.

"Thanks for coming, She loves you so much. She looked better last night than she has since before the heart attack." His eyes glazed over, and his body slumped just slightly. Noel felt her heart lurch instantly wanting to take his pain away.

"I love her too," Noel said suddenly shy.

Jesse glanced up looking across the street, "I just wanted to come by and said hi. I know last night was weird but...I... I'm really glad you're here."

"Me too," she said barely a whisper.

"My gallery's just across the street, right there." He pointed to a building that used to be a general store long before she was born.

The classy black awning simply read, *Wellings Art Gallery*. She could see many pieces of art displayed in the large glass windows. His keen artistic eye brought life and elegance to the abandoned building.

"It looks great, Jess." His heart caught in his chest when she said his name. It seemed so normal to be talking to her as if time had not robbed them of the special time they could've shared. *Time wasn't the real culprit*, he thought bitterly.

He reached through the window and touched her hand. Goosebumps ran up her arm and a shiver down her spine. "Ah, it's cold," he shook his shoulders misreading her body's reaction. "You better go, um, I'll see you soon."

"See you later." Noel put her car into reverse and pulled away quickly so not to run into anyone else. Jimmy had been nice, Cassandra unpleasant, but running into Jesse Wellings had been downright painful. She needed to get back home and sit where it was nice and quiet.

Quiet, unfortunately, was not something Noel received that day as she was greeted by a most excited Marta.

"Oh Miss. Noel, I'm so glad you made it back safe. Of course, town is only five minutes away, but I've been lonely. Mr. W's been in his study for hours. He sits in there and cries sometimes. His heart's broken. I suppose it's nice to have someone love you that much, don't you think? Do you know if I were to get sick right now not one person would mind? Not one! Can you imagine it?"

On and on the girl chattered away until she had to make lunch. Noel used that moment to visit Mrs. Wellings.

"Mama Jay," Noel spoke into the room using the old nickname she used for Jana when she was a girl. "You awake?"

"Yes, my girl, come in. John said you'd read to me today. I do fancy some Great Expectations myself, what do you think?" The older woman flashed a genuine smile.

"I'd like that very much. I haven't read Great Expectations in a long time. Maybe we can get a few chapters in before Speedy gets lunch done." Noel unsuccessfully concealed a grin.

"So, you've gotten acquainted with Marta?" Mrs. Wellings laughed weakly for several seconds holding her side.

"That I have," Noel giggled as she looked over the bookcase for Great Expectations. "It's a wonder the girl doesn't turn blue from lack of oxygen."

Pulling the ragged, much-loved book from its usual place on the oak bookshelf, Noel hugged the leather-bound book to her chest. The bookshelf and all those sweet books had been her haven, her escape since she was a little girl. Jana always allowed Noel passage inside the master bedroom to borrow her books, as she pleased.

Laughing harder Jana croaks, "Oh honey, but I swear to it she does! I've seen it with my own two eyes!"

Once the pair had contained their giggles, Noel sat by Jana on her bed and said, "I've missed you so much."

"I missed you too, but no time to dwell on the past love. Let's just enjoy the present. Come sit close to me and read."

Snuggling close to the older woman's side Noel began the epic adventure of Pip, the boy Noel so related to when she was a child, although his aunt and uncle were a great deal more involved in his life than her parents had ever been in hers. Noel felt a great attachment to the boy. She still struggled with finding her place in the world. Would she ever succeed?

Jana laid her head on Noel's shoulder, her breathing becoming shallower as the girl read. Once sure that Momma Jay was asleep, Noel laid her head against Jana's and she too dozed off.

CHAPTER FOURTEEN

Jesse found Noel and his mother asleep leaned against each other. They looked so peaceful that he hated to wake them. A tug at his heart reminded him he'd made Noel leave; he had hurt her. If his mother knew the part he played in that, he'd die of shame.

"Noel," he whispered lightly touching her shoulder. She opened her eyes and turned to him, a warm smile on her face.

Jesse. Once her brain recognized who he was and that she was still mad at him, her smile faded.

"What time is it?" She asked yawning.

"Almost time for dinner. Go get ready while I help Momma up," he said, holding his hand out to help her up.

"Okay," sliding out of the bed, ignoring his offer of help, she tried unsuccessfully to not wake Jana.

"Oh goodness, did we fall asleep? Jesse? Did you come for dinner again? Well the Lord surely rains his blessings on me. My favorite girl and boy home under the same roof twice in one week."

Noel slid out of the room to freshen up for dinner while Jesse spent time with his mother. "Yes Momma, I'm here. Let me help you up."

Noel closed the door behind her and leaned her head against the door listening for a moment.

"You two okay?" Jana asked weakly.

Jesse let out a deep breath, "I wish I knew Momma, she just–"

A nasally voice sounded from behind Noel. "Jesse in there?" Sara Rhymes stood at the other end of the hall, hands on hips, watching Noel eavesdrop.

"Yes, he um, he's helping her get ready for–"

Sara interrupted, "I thought that's what you were for."

"I uh, I'm sorry?" Noel asked wondering what Sara was speaking of.

"Didn't you swoop in here in their time of need to make sure you make it into Jana's will?" Sara's perfect little face folded into a sour grimace.

Noel shook her head dumbly. "Her will?"

"Don't play with me, sugar. Jesse and I've sacrificed every Monday since we've been together to…"

"Sacrificed? You and Jesse have *sacrificed*?? Way to go! Congratulations!" Noel clapped her hands lightly. "You want a pat on the back for…*for what?* Coming to dinner once a week? Like she's some kind of obligation? What kind of person are you?" Noel's voice grew louder, and her head started to wave from side to side in sassy anger. "I have no idea why Jesse would allow someone like you to even darken the door–"

"Noel? What's up?" Jesse stepped out of Mrs. Wellings bedroom ushering his mother into the hallway. His dark eyes looked from Sara to Noel, his face drawn in confusion.

"Oh darling," Sara's face fell into an exaggerated pout. "She was being just terrible to me. All I asked was why she suddenly had such an interest in this family. Jesse, I'm afraid she's using y'all."

"Using us for what, exactly?" Jana asked, her breathing labored.

"Oh Jana, you poor dear," Sara's pout drawing into a grimace of pain. "How foolish we are keeping you standing here when you should be resting." Sara grabbed at Jana's arm.

Jana pulled away gently. "I can make it to the table myself, thank you. Come Noel, I may need you as a buffer between me and Marta. I'm not entirely sure I have enough energy for that ray of sunshine today."

Nodding, Noel placed her hand on Jana's back guiding her into the dining area. Behind her Noel could hear Jesse and Sara speaking in hushed tones.

CHAPTER FIFTEEN

She'd been ten, maybe eleven when Jesse drug her to his house to show her 'something special.'

"What is it Jesse? I was just about to talk Mrs. Jones into some ice cream." Noel growled as Jesse snagged her up from Mrs. Jones yard with promises of 'something special.'

"Just be patient for once in your life," Jesse walked as if he were an Olympic speed walker. "I have Popsicles at the house. You can have one later."

'Fine, but this better be good Jesse Wellings, because Mrs. Jones had those sherbet push-up ice creams, and they're my favorite. I didn't even have to pull weeds for it neither!"

"Geez, I'll never understand why I didn't pick a boy to be my best friend," Jesse muttered.

"Cause next to me they are plain, boring, and dumb, and you know it!" Noel said, streaking past Jesse and tapping him on the back of his head with her knuckles.

Laughing, Jesse ran to keep up. Yes, compared to Noel, all kids were commonplace.

"Woohoo! Dang, before long I won't be able to keep up with you." Noel panted. "Your legs are longer than my whole body!"

Jesse chuckled, "Yeah, Momma said I'm gonna be a giant if I don't quit growing."

"Well I'm two inches shy of being a dwarf!" Noel shouted to the sky shaking her fists at the heavens. Jesse laughed.

Noel's eyes grew round with seriousness, "Its true! We looked it up in Mrs. Murphy's class."

"That chart's for adults. You'll grow, I promise ya." Noel looked hesitant for a minute.

"Well if I don't. I'm gonna beat you for giving me false hope!" She shot him a warning look.

"You'd have to catch me first!" and with that, Jesse streaked into his house. Noel was right behind him.

He ran through the living room, hooked a right down the hallway, and straight into the guest room. Noel followed quickly on his heels ready, to give him a tiny pounding for beating her.

When she entered the room, she stopped dead in her tracks, her eyes widened in astonishment. The room which had once been sparsely decorated looked much different. "What's this?" She asked.

"Well," Mrs. Wellings said from behind. "We had the room remodeled."

"Oops, sorry Momma Jay," Noel said hoping she and Jesse wouldn't get scolded for running in the house. She had no idea that Mrs. Wellings would be in the room. Not only was Mrs. Wellings in the room, so was her husband.

"Well it's awfully nice. Y'all did a good job making this room real pretty." Noel said politely.

The room had been beautifully decorated. The walls were painted a muted shade of blush. A small cloud-like mattress was cloaked in a white lace bedspread. The bedding was adorned with pillows of assorted shapes and sizes in various shades of pink. A small white desk and chair sat in the far corner of the room. Her favorite piece of furniture was the white chest of drawers with tiny pink roses etched into the wood. Atop the dresser were some of Noel's favorite books.

"I wish I had a room like this!" Noel exclaimed.

Mrs. Wellings looked to her husband. "Noel," she said crouching down to be eye level with the girl. Noel turned her big gray eyes to the woman. "I hope you don't find us silly for doing this but...this room is for you."

"Will I live here?" Noel asked excitedly.

Mrs. Wellings sighed. "Not exactly," Noel's body sagged just a little.

"But...I've spoken with your father, and he's agreed that when...the fighting gets too bad at home...you can come stay with us for the night. You don't have to ask, you just come over and let me know you're here."

Mrs. Wellings made her best attempt at a smile, but her body still burned with anger at the thought of her last encounter with the Miracles. Mr. Miracle himself suggested that Mr. Wellings should pay them to keep their daughter.

Trying not to bite back too hard, Mrs. Wellings struck a deal. She'd refrain from calling the police on them for child neglect if Noel were allowed to eat a good meal at night in the Wellings home, and if she could stay over when the drinking got out of hand.

Threats of law enforcement seemed to put Mr. Miracle in his place rather quickly. It brought to question whether there were illegal activity going on in the home as well. However, if Jana could keep Noel safe and far from the state orphanage, then she'd do all in her power to save the child.

"Oh wow! That's at least five nights a week!" Noel jumped up and down with excitement.

"Your father also said you can come here and have dinner with us every night if you want."

"Oh, man! Did you hear that Jess! We can be together always!" Noel and Jesse held hands and jumped up and down with excitement.

"I know! See mom, I kept a good secret, didn't I?" Jesse asked looking to his mother.

"You did love, you did a very good job. Now, you two go play until supper please." Mrs. Wellings voice grew thick. She was able to hold the tears back long enough for the pair to make it to the back yard.

Mr. Wellings walked past his wife and pulled the curtain panel in Noel's new room back, so he could watch the kids play.

"I don't know if God sent her to us or if He sent us to her." He said.

"I believe a little of both," Jana answered grabbing her husband's hand, watching the two children who brought her life meaning.

CHAPTER SIXTEEN

Marta set the table with the china that Mrs. Wellings normally reserved for guests. It was an old Willow pattern her mother gifted her before she passed away. Marta had made a beautiful roast, homemade bread, potatoes, and fresh green beans. Noel wanted to appreciate the spread, but her hands still shook after her altercation with Sara.

Jana could see Noel was quite shaken. "Don't worry about Sara, she's not worth getting upset over."

Noel sighed heavily, "You don't believe what she said, do you?"

"Goodness no! It wouldn't matter anyway. You've been in my will since you were a tiny thing, and that'll never change."

"But I don't want anything—" Noel started.

"It's not about what you want, dear," Jana patted Noel's hand. "Here, set me at the end of the table. That way, I won't be tempted to spill my drink on Ms. Sara's pretty white pants."

"It won't stop me," muttered Marta coming from behind.

Jana chuckled, "Now, now, Marta. What do we say about folks like Ms. Sara?"

Marta blew breath through her lips loudly, "People like that have no real joy in their lives and should be pitied."

"That's right dear. Now, could you find Mr. W and let him know dinner is done?" Jana asked.

"Sure thing!" Marta said zooming down the hall brushing past Jesse and Sara.

"There's something not right with her," Sara mumbled.

Jesse and Sara walked into the dining room where everyone else had gathered. Sara looked at Noel.

"Noel," Sara started, false kindness permeated in her words. "I hope you'll accept my apology for being so brash with you a moment ago. I just…" Her eyes welled with tears. "I just love this family and–I want to protect them. I'm sure you understand." Her words were kind but lacked sincerity.

Noel smiled, ready to make peace so as not to upset Jana. "Of course, I understand, you're right. I've been gone a long time. If I were you, I'd think the same thing."

Sara turned to Jesse who nervously watched the exchange, "See Jess, I told you she'd be reasonable., You worry over nothing."

Jesse's face turned red as Noel cut her eyes to him.

Did he think I'd be unreasonable? Of course, he'd think I couldn't handle myself. She thought.

Noel opened her mouth to let Jesse know she could handle a great deal more than he thought, but Jana stopped her.

"Oh Noel, I meant to tell you!" Jana lightly touched Noel's arm. Raising her eyebrows Noel looked at Jana in surprise.

"Jimmy Wren from the pharmacy called. He was interested in how you've been doing and if…if you might be seeing anyone."

Noel choked on air, not expecting Jana to be so bold in front of Jesse and his girlfriend.

"Oh my," Mr. Wellings said entering the room, he grabbed the water pitcher from the table and poured Noel a glass. "Here, have some water."

"You okay?" He asked. Noel wiped a napkin across her face to dry the tears that streaked down her cheeks.

"Yes, sorry. Just swallowed air down the wrong pipe." Noel answered, smiling gratefully at Mr. Wellings. She shot Jana a teary look.

"You need more water?" He asked.

"No, but maybe I will excuse myself for a moment." Before anyone could say anything, further, Noel excused herself from the table. She needed to throw some cool water on her face and to absorb the words Jana had said.

Why would Jimmy Wren want to know her dating status?

CHAPTER SEVENTEEN

Noel snuggled deep into her fleece-lined coat. It had started snowing–just tiny flakes, but snow nonetheless. She loved watching the flakes fall through the night sky. In the distance, the hills of Kentucky towered above. She hoped they'd have a white Christmas. The holiday was less than two weeks away, but after living in Kentucky long enough, one learns the weather can be quite unpredictable. summer, fall, and winter weather can all occur in the same week. Noel had come to believe that spring was nothing more than just a myth.

"Hey," Jesse said finding Noel on the back patio. "I thought I would find you here." When they were younger, he would find her on the back patio just taking in the beauty of the land that surrounded them. It was her way of unwinding.

"Hey," she said back. "Where's Sara?"

Noel glanced around on high alert for the evil beauty queen.

"I sent her back to her place for the time being. She doesn't like to visit for long, and I feel like with each passing day, I should be here more and more. I'm scared for mom, you know?"

"Yeah," Noel said not sure what else to say.

"I'm sorry Sara was awful to you earlier. She's just..." Jesse tried to make excuses for his bratty lady.

"What do you see in her anyway? She's not nice, Jesse, you deserve–"

"What do you think I deserve exactly?" He shot back.

"Better," Noel answered. "Definitely better."

Jesse struggled to find words to say. "She's beautiful, she's…"

Noel waited in silence, eager to prove her point. Yes, Sara was beautiful...from what Noel had witnessed so far, that was her *only* positive quality.

Nervously, he ran his hand through his hair. "What about Jim?" he joked trying to lighten the mood.

Noel chuckled, "I was so not ready to hear that. I don't know really. I saw him for the first time today that the pharmacy."

"Are you interested, or is there someone where you live now?" He asked, secretly hoping she'd say no to both.

Noel rolled her eyes and shook her head. "No, I tend to attract the wrong sort, so I've sworn off men for a while."

Jesse was glad of her answer. Jealousy boiled inside his stomach thinking of Noel dating. He pushed his anger down. *Don't think of her that way, it can only lead to trouble.* "I'm going to say goodnight to mom and head home soon. Don't forget to stop by the gallery one day. I think you'll like what we've done with the place."

A burning desire to beg him to stay filled Noel's being. It'd been a long time since she experienced the comfort that came with being around him. She missed it. She missed him. She missed who they were together.

"I will…See ya later." She half waved her hand, not looking his way. She didn't want him to see how badly she wanted him to stay. It was better if she didn't get too close. It could only lead to more heartache.

Jesse looked at Noel for several seconds. She didn't look back. After a few painful moments of silence, he went inside.

She didn't realize she had been holding her breath until he left, then she began to breathe again. It took several deep, chilled breaths to steady her rapidly beating heart. She stayed outside, waiting until she heard the engine of his pickup rumble to life before she went back inside to get ready for bed.

CHAPTER EIGHTEEN

He had everything. His life had finally fallen back into place. The memories of her lived in the back of his mind, where they belonged. But now she was back and those memories, those feelings flooded his entire being and now there was — more.

More.

But there was also Sara. Sara was gorgeous; there wasn't a flaw anywhere to be seen. She kept him straight. She'd helped him pick up the pieces of his broken heart when he accepted he'd lost Noel forever.

He'd taken Noel for granted, thinking she'd be there always. How was he to know what losing her would do to him? He had just been a kid back then.

He tried to convince himself that he loved her like a sister. Convincing himself that anything other than a platonic relationship would ruin them. What if things got weird, what if it ruined everything? He kept her at arm's length, and she didn't push herself on him.

When she left town, it tore his heart in two, and he was convinced he'd never love again. Until Sara came along. Sara was pushy and forward-thinking, keeping him on his toes. She was beautiful and had goals for herself, for the gallery, and even for him.

She made him happy, and he thought that was enough until he laid eyes on Noel again. Her sweet, innocent beauty drew him in. When he stood next to her in the kitchen he had to fight his body not to wrap her in his arms and profess his undying love for her.

Thank God his dad walked in when he did, or who knows what he would've done.

CHAPTER NINETEEN

Noel stood at the double doors of the Wellings' bedroom, her hand raised to knock on the door. She wanted to pepper Jana with questions about Jesse and his woman, but she also didn't want to know. How serious were they? Did Jana think they'd get married?

"Momma Jay, are you awake?" Noel whispered.

Jana's eyes, though heavy, were open. "Yes, I'm awake and feeling terrible about earlier."

Noel rose her eyebrows and looked at the woman whose pale cheeks were turning a grayish pink. "Oh, what for?" Noel tried to act coy, but she smiled giving Jana a hard time. She could never be mean to Jana, she was too sweet.

"I thought since I might be dying, you'd cut me some slack and not make me give a full-out apology." Jana chided the girl.

"Not a chance," Noel grinned.

"Fine," Jana crossed her arms across her chest. "I saw your mouth drop, ready to lay into Jesse, and I just knew I had to stop you. There's something between you and my son but discussing it in front of Sara Rhymes would be a mistake. Now, I've never pressed you about why you don't come home anymore or why you and Jesse no longer have a relationship. But I do believe now is the time for you two to have a little talk."

"Maybe discussing it would be a mistake." Noel said closing herself off.

"So, would bottling it up…" Jana paused searching for the right words. "Noel, did my son…did he take make inappropriate advances at you when you were teens?"

The way she asked tore at Noel's heart. "Of course not! Jesse's too good for that…it's silly and something I need to get over. Don't worry, Jesse and I'll be fine." Noel didn't believe her own words, but she wanted Jana to believe them.

"Why would you ask if Jesse had taken advantage of me?" Noel ask curiosity getting the best of her.

"When I mentioned Jimmy Wren had called asking about you, a look of jealousy crossed his face. I thought maybe he felt he has some claim to you…maybe something I didn't know about. I mean I hoped he'd never…but people are people, and they make mistakes."

Noel shook her head. "Jesse and I are fine. Now get some sleep Momma Jay. Pops said your nurse is coming in the morning."

"Fine, but we'll talk about this again. And about that Jimmy Wren–he's awfully good looking, isn't he?" The older woman giggled.

"Good night Momma Jay," Noel laughed making her way to the door.

"Good night sweetheart," Jana said mischief gleaming in her sleep deprived eyes.

Noel shut the door and sagged against it wishing that Momma Jay had been right and that Jesse looked at her with anything other than friendship in his eyes.

CHAPTER TWENTY

"Psst, psst," the noise grew louder. Noel snuggled deeper into the fluffy down comforter, sinking further into the cloud she slept upon.

"Mm, goo– "Noel mumbled, swatting at the being who threatened to pull her from her peaceful slumber.

"Psst...Miss Noel, psst," the hushed voice of Marta buzzed in her ear.

"What is it Marta?" Noel asked propping herself up on her elbows suddenly alert. "What's wrong?"

"Sorry to wake you Miss, but I... I don't know who else to speak with and I thought maybe you'd understand what I have to say." Marta's eyes glistened with tears that threatened to spill down her cheeks.

Sitting up Noel looked at the wiry young lady. "What is it? Is Jana..." Noel's heart thudded in her chest. She was afraid to finish the thought.

"No, Mrs. W's fine, sleeping peacefully. I checked on her myself. It's...it's that Sara Rhymes who has me all wound up. Mr. And Mrs. W both say you and Jesse are good friends and well...maybe you can tell him that he's making a mistake. She's not right for Jesse. It's a terrible burden for Mrs. W."

"Marta," Noel started with a sigh of relief. "I can't...Jesse and I—we aren't friends anymore. I mean I'll always care for him, but we were childhood friends. Now, we'd barely pass as acquaintances."

"I don't know Miss, maybe time has gotten in the way, but true friendships aren't so easily broken." Marta's eyes grew big. Noel was afraid Marta was putting too much faith in the pull she had with her old comrade.

"Yes, but it's different with Jesse and I…there is too much water under the bridge…" Noel said with a yawn. "Can we discuss this at another time? Its…" Noel checked her phone. "Marta, its 4:30 in the morning!"

"Well, I like to get started early," Marta sniffed indignantly.

"I'm sure you do...I, however…I'm going back to bed. Goodnight," Noel pulled the cover back up to her chin.

Standing to leave, Marta turned to Noel. Light from the moon illuminated her face. "If you care for Mr. Jesse, for all of them, you should say something."

"Goodnight Marta," Noel turned away. Why was it her problem who Jesse dated? He was a grown man—a grown man who could make his own decisions.

Marta paused, then accepted the dismissal. Her shoulders slumped as she slid out the door. Noel burrowed deep into her bed hoping to find sleep again; however thoughts of Jesse, Sara, and Jana floated through her mind keeping sleep at arm's length.

*   *   *

"Pops?" Noel stuck her head into Mr. Wellings' study.

"Hey, how's our girl?" Mr. Wellings' bloodshot eyes cried for sleep.

"I suppose I'd be better if my eyes weren't deceiving me. Surely, you aren't neglecting to take care of yourself, now are you?" Noel looked around the room surprised by the chaos she saw there. Piles of paperwork lay haphazardly all over his desk. She could see his trash can was overfilled and cups of old coffee littered the other free spaces.

"Oh, don't worry about me, I'll be fine. Just need a nap—" the man said rubbing his wrinkled hand across his face as if to shake the sleep away.

"You need more than a nap. You'll do no one any good if you let yourself go. Momma Jay needs you. Jesse needs you." She scolded.

"Nah, Jess is all grown up'" Mr. Wellings picked up an old coffee cup, looked down at its contents, then put it back down.

"That's not true!" Noel's raspy voice grew thick.

Pops chuckled, "You're right, sorry about that. Can you forgive a silly old man who has been sulking over the misfortunes life has thrown his way?"

Noel smiled softly, "I'll allow it this once, but only if you start caring for yourself a little better."

"You sound like Jana," he growled.

"She's a smart lady. I'll take that as a compliment. Now, I need to run some errands. I must go to the library and back to the drug store for some items I forgot to pack. Can I get you anything?"

"No dear, I believe I'll go rest with Jana for a while. Tonight we'll order in something for dinner. Marta's off this evening so we must fend for ourselves."

"Speaking of Marta, should I send her in here to clean up a bit?" Noel asked looking at the filthy room, disappointed the efficient housekeeper had not touched the room.

"No," he shook his head. "She's not allowed in here. She'd tell Jana how I've let it go. I'll take care of it later."

"No, you're going to rest. I'm going to go to town, and while I'm out I'll grab a few things to cook dinner for you and Momma Jay. When I get back, I am cleaning this room, mister, so if you have anything important you may want to put it aside so I don't toss it out."

Mr. Wellings opened his mouth to object.

"No arguing," she overruled him. "I'll have Marta bring lunch back to you both, so you can have one free day to rest."

"I want to argue–" Mr. Wellings said his head drooping. He was exhausted; taking care of his wife had robbed him of his strength.

"It'd do you no good Pops," Noel said. "Now, grab a shower, and a cozy set of pj's, then take a much-needed nap. Got it, sir?" Noel chided walking from the room.

Mr. Wellings shook his head, speaking to the empty room. "When did I become the child?"

CHAPTER TWENTY-ONE

The store was packed with people that afternoon. Noel smiled, pleased that the pharmacy still did so well. Jana shared with her that a chain drug store had opened on the other side of town, and she was afraid the tiny shop wouldn't be able to compete. However, thanks to loyal customers and apparently, a good owner, the pharmacy held its own.

"Noel," Jimmy called from across the store. "How are you?"

"Oh good! I'm glad you're here! I had to pick up a few things–and to be honest, I needed to get out of the house for a bit. I'm used to being on my own most the time so being in a house around people twenty-four hours a day can be a little overwhelming." She confessed.

"Yeah, I can understand that." Jimmy agreed. Secretly, he would do anything to have a home filled with people, he had been alone far too long.

"So, have you–" Noel started.

"Oh good, Noel." Sara Rhymes drawled from behind. Noel and Jimmy turned to the striking young woman dressed in a sharp black business suit. Her long dark hair was twisted high in a tight bun, not a hair out of place. Both Jimmy and Noel inwardly cringed. Sara looked so out of place with the other residents that milled around the store. "I just wanted you to know Jesse and I'd be over for dinner tomorrow night. Hopefully, you and I can get to know one another better."

Sara narrowed her ice blue eyes on Noel. Noel refrained from rolling her own. *I get it, keep your enemies close…*Noel thought to herself. *Why am I such a threat to this woman?*

"Well, isn't that fantastic? It's so nice to add an extra day to your weekly visit to the Wellings." Noel said evenly.

"Better than your, what…once every six years?" Sara shot back the devil in her eyes.

Jimmy stepped in between the ladies, feeling the tension escalate. "Sorry Sara, Noel's joining me for dinner tomorrow. We haven't seen each other in ages. You girls will have to catch up another day."

"Oh, is that so? Well, another time will have to do then." Sara smiled, a gesture that should have increased her looks but instead drew her face into a look of mild discomfort.

Noel clenched her teeth together. "Of course, another time."

"Humph, yes, another time." Sara sauntered off after she gave Jimmy a quick glance over, a smile rising her face. Every male head in the joint turned their heads watching her exit the building.

"Later," Jimmy mumbled, turning his attention back to Noel.

"So, dinner?" She raised her brows in question.

He shared a large toothy smile and shrugged. "Just trying to help ya out."

Rubbing the back of his neck with his massive hand he asked, "Is that okay? I mean…it's me or Mrs. Rhymes—"

Noel laughed, "It's more than okay. I'd love to have dinner with you. Where do you want to meet?"

"Um, well I'd planned to fire up the grill and make some steaks. Do you feel comfortable coming to my place?" Pink crept up his face past his beard.

Noel nodded and lightly tapped his arm, "Sure, that sounds great. Where do you live?"

The color on Jimmy's cheeks brightened, "Up Old Mountain road, you know Bob Kilmer's old place?"

"Yes, I know exactly where it's at." Noel's eyes grew big.

Old Mountain Road was a windy gravel road that cut straight through the hills of Harm County. Each wooden cabin built for luxury. The homes were situated far enough away from the road and each other that one could not see their neighbors. Ancient oak and pine trees covered the grounds. It was a little slice of heaven as far as Noel was concerned.

The cabins were much different than the beat-up shack Noel grew up in at the bottom of the hills, when she wasn't with the Wellings. As a little girl, she'd sneak outside while her parents fought through the night and watch the mountain light up as the residents of each log home returned from their daily lives. She dreamed of having a place like that to live one day. Unfortunately, on a teacher's salary that wasn't likely to happen.

"Great, see you tomorrow...say 7-ish?" Jimmy asked raising his eyebrows.

"Seven is perfect, see you then." Noel ducked her head shyly.

"Until then, my lady!" Jimmy bowed then rushed off. His face all the way up to his forehead was a perfect shade of crimson. Noel watched his broad shoulders retreat. *What just happened?* She asked herself.

*   *   *

It was nice to walk back into the Wellings home after a few hours out in town. Noel was able to visit the library and some local shops without running into anyone else she knew. She needed some downtime and was glad she had gone out. Plus, she had a date with Jimmy Wren!

"Momma Jay? You're up!" Noel exclaimed. She was delighted to see Jana sitting up in her easy chair in the living room. She had a hardcover book in her lap and a cozy fire crackling in the fireplace.

"Oh good, you're back!" Jana called. "How was your day? Oh my, what's happened? Your cheeks are flush." The older woman's eyes twinkled.

"They are?" Noel's fingers touched her face. "Well...you know how Jimmy called and asked about me yesterday?"

"Mmhmm," Jana sat up straighter and leaned towards the girl.

"He asked me to dinner...for tomorrow night." Noel blurted.

"That does sound lovely." Jana smiled at the girl, slightly disappointed that it was Jimmy and not Jesse that Noel had a date with.

"Yes, I'm sure it'll be nice–" Noel drifted off.

"But?" Jana prodded.

"But, I'm here to care for you not go out on dates–" A pang of guilt rocked her gut.

"Wait," Jana held her hand up to stop Noel. "I didn't ask you here to "care" for me. We have Marta, my nurse, and my husband for that. I just want you here, at home. Just knowing you're asleep under my roof every night is a huge comfort. So please, do us all a favor and don't feel like you must nurse me to health, cater to me, or provide endless entertainment."

Noel looked away, "Okay, sorry, I will try to relax."

"Wonderful! Now, tell me what you plan to wear?" Jana asked, excitement building for Noel's upcoming date.

CHAPTER TWENTY-TWO

High School

She was running late for class when her bookbag split at the seams causing her belongings to scatter across the hallway. Pens, pencils, folders–all her homework and notes littered the ground. Great, just what she needed. Mr. Bailey was going to make a fool of her in front of the class if she were tardy again. First period was always the worst. She couldn't wake up early when she stayed at her own home at night.

Her mom and dad had been up fighting like crazy – as usual – keeping her up well past two a.m. She should've stayed with the Wellings, but she'd been keeping her distance from Jess for a while. Her feelings towards him had shifted, and she was confused on how she felt about it and even worse how he'd feel about it.

"Hey girl," Cassandra gushed, standing over Noel as she watched her pick her belongings up. Noel gave her half a glance. She was in her cheer uniform and as usual, she looked amazing. The new black and white uniform fit the girl's form like a glove, accentuating her curves. Noel sucked in a breath pushing down her jealousy while trying not to compare herself to Cassandra.

Cassandra didn't offer to help as she chatted away. "Who're you going to the Christmas formal with?"

Suddenly very interested in her broken bookbag, Noel shrugged. "I dunno, no one—maybe…I'm not into dances and stuff…"

"What? That's crazy talk! Come on now! Everyone has to go. I'm head of the formal committee, and I say you must go!" Cassandra's sweet southern voice dripped with sass.

"I…I maybe I'll just go stag…like with friends." She wanted to tell someone so badly, how she felt, but to tell Cassandra would be to tell the whole school. She had the biggest mouth ever, and yet she had this way about her that made you instantly tell her your deepest secrets.

"Girl, don't hold it in, just tell me. I can see it written all over your face, there's a boy. Is it someone I know?" Cassandra put her hands on her hips and cocked her head to one side, her hair falling in perfect red spirals over her shoulder. Noel wished she had that confidence.

Shoving her belongings in the broken bag she stood to face Cassandra. Noel nodded, giving in. Cassandra's eyes lit up like a Christmas tree. "Tell me, tell me, tell me!" She wrapped her tiny hands around Noel's arm and jumped up and down, a Cheshire grin creeping up her face. Juicy gossip.

"I thought maybe…Jesse would go…just as friends of course, but—" Noel's pale cheeks instantly lit up, she wished she hadn't said a word.

"Shut up! You like Jesse Wellings? I thought you like lived with his family or something. Wait! Y'all ain't related, are you?" Cassandras eyes widened hoping for the juiciest piece of gossip since Mr. Dean caught Mr. Elmore with the school secretary in the janitor's closet.

"No! I mean, I sta-stay there sometimes when my mom and dad—when things aren't good at home…" Noel trailed off not ready to share her family life with Cassandra. She'd already shared one secret she wished she could take back.

"How're you going to ask him?" The red-headed beauty asked the corner of her eyes squinting just slightly.

Noel's eyes dimmed, "I mean, I probably won't, what if he said no? We've been friends most our lives, I don't want to ruin that."

"Ruin it? Honey you only live once! Here, I'll tell you what. Let me ask him for you. That'll keep you from feeling so awkward." Cassandra offered clapping her hands in delight.

Noel studied the girl who had more self-confidence than Noel could ever imagine. She was cheer captain, bubbly, dated only the cutest boys, and her parents were loaded, so of course she cruised around town in a brand-spanking-new, white BMW. Noel supposed if she had everything Cassandra did, she'd have little fear when it came to asking a boy to the Christmas formal.

"I..." Noel shook her head no.

"Really girl, it's no problem. I have lunch period with him. I'll do it in private, so no one hears. Then I'll find you in between classes and let you know what he says. If he says no, it will be just between me, you, and Jesse. How does that sound?" Cassandra pushed.

"Are you sure?" Noel fiddled with her hair, staring blankly at the ground. What was she doing?

"Of course, I'm sure! Jesse Wellings would be a fool to not go to the dance with you. With the right makeup, a bit more confidence, and seriously, with your pale skin, a bright red dress would set your eyes off, driving them boys crazy! You could have any guy you wanted, well those that matter anyways. Believe me when I say you are a certified, hottie girl." Cassandra did a little head wave and finger snap.

Noel blushed but giggled at Cassandra's bold ways. "You really think so?"

Cassandra grabbed Noel's hands in hers, "Trust me, I know boys."

Taking in a deep breath Noel sighed loudly. "You know what, go for it!"

Cassandra clapped her hands, "YAY! You won't regret it. See ya later, lovie!"

Over head the tardy bell rang causing Noel to dash down the hall to class, thoughts of Cassandra and Jess pushed from her mind, for the moment.

*   *   *

Nervously, Noel fiddled with her pen wondering what Jesse would say...what would he think? She was a fool; she never should've told Cassandra anything!

"Noel, could you be a dear and run this note down to the guidance office please?" Mrs. Tracy asked breaking through Noel's thoughts.

"Okay," she agreed, eagerly taking the folded paper into her hands.

"Here take the hall pass." Mrs. Tracy handed her a giant pencil with a tag that read *Hall Pass*. Noel hated when teachers used big items for passes, but she supposed it kept them from getting lost or stolen as often.

Walking quickly through the building, Noel decided the fastest way to the office was to cut through the back hall that led around the back side of the cafeteria. She could hear the loud voices and laughter of her peers who were already enjoying their lunch. A pang of nervousness hit her gut as she realized that any moment Cassandra would talk to Jesse for her.

She wondered what he would say. What if he said yes? Would that be the start of a new phase in their relationship? She could picture him picking her up in a limo, both the best dressed and most precious couple at the dance. He would hold her close when the D.J. played slow songs. Would he kiss her then?

Her stomach twisted into a hard knot. It was too much. How would she ever make it through the next hour to find out what he said. What if he said no? What if it ruined everything?

She turned the corner to the cafeteria, the office just doors away, when she heard Cassandra's voice and saw she was speaking to Jesse. Well, Jesse and half the football team. *Oh no, not here,* she thought. *What are you doing Cassandra?* Quickly, she stepped back straining to hear what they said over the chatter that drifted from the overcrowded lunch room.

Cassandra chuckled. "You're so funny! Oh, by the way Jess, you should watch out. Noel has a thing for you."

Several chuckles and a few cat calls could be heard. "Way to go Jess," someone jeered.

"What? Noel? No, we're just friends…were best–"

"Not to her you're not, in her mind there's something more," Cassandra cut across his words taunting him.

Jesse chuckled, "I think you got the wrong idea. She and I–"

"Your family lets her stay all night, right?" Cassandra flirted. *What was she doing?* Noel thought, rage boiling inside her like lava.

"Well yeah, but–" he interjected.

"You and she spend a lot of time together alone, right?" Cassandra spoke louder to be heard over the boys howling and catcalls.

"Yes, but that don't mean…listen there's nothing between Noel and me. My family and I we…we feel sorry for her. Her dad's a drunk and her mom's so strung out she don't even know who Noel is half the time."

"Tough break man," a male's voice sad with mock sadness "So if you don't want her, can I take a shot at her?" Jesse gave the boy a warning look but said nothing.

"Maybe they're already fooling around," Noel recognized Blake Livers' voice and unmistakable hyena-like chuckle. She hated his chuckle and his lack of grammar skills.

Tears burned Noel's eyes, how could he? How could they? Those kids were making fun of her. They were kids she knew. She had grown up with them. They were kids she had been more than kind to.

"My mom forces me to hang with her, it's hard to shake her...she doesn't have any other friends. I feel sorry for her." Jesse looked from Cassandra to the guys who surrounded them. He looked like a trapped animal.

Noel stepped around the corner. He was handsome standing there, so tall and strong in his Letterman jacket. He'd grown the top of his hair a little longer, and it partly covered one eye. She'd caught him practicing how to flip it effortlessly from his eyes once and made fun of him unmercifully for a week. However, right now she wanted to pull him bald.

Jesse instantly sensed her presence, anger drifted from her body hitting him in intense waves. Their eyes locked. Tears streamed freely down her cheeks. His face fell, and his heart crumbled, littering his chest with pieces of tiny heart confetti. *What had he done?*

"Oopsie," Cassandra giggled covering her red painted lips with her hand. "I think that's a no on the formal front, kiddo. Sorry." Cassandra giggled, her peach colored lips pouted in mock sympathy.

To keep from beating Jesse with the giant pencil hall pass, Noel bolted. "Noel, wait!" Jesse cried taking a step to go after her.

Cassandra hooked her arm through his stopping him in his tracks. "Let her cool down. If you go to her now, it'll only make things worse."

She was right. Jesse had felt the brunt of Noel's anger a few times, and it wasn't pretty. She needed time to cool off. Looking down the hallway, Jesse nodded and grudgingly walked to the lunchroom with Cassandra and the rest of his crew. He'd talk to Noel later, and things would be okay. They were best friends after all. Nothing could break that.

CHAPTER TWENTY-THREE

Nervously, Noel smoothed down her top and flicked the stray strands of hair behind her ear. She had spent an over an hour getting ready that night hoping Jimmy would notice. He was different than the other guys she had dated, and she wanted to look nice for him.

The one thing that Noel took from her past was Cassandra's advice on wearing red. The holly colored top really did make her eyes pop and was a pretty contrast to her platinum blond locks and porcelain skin.

"Oh my, look at you Miss Noel! A true beauty," Marta gushed when Noel walked into the dining area to collect her coat.

"Thank you, Marta," Noel couldn't conceal the grin that crossed her face at the lady's praise.

"Mr. Jesse, come look at Miss Noel!" Marta called behind her. Noel's heart stopped at mention of his name.

Jesse stepped out of the kitchen. He had to fight himself not to stand there like an idiot with his mouth wide open. Stopping dead in his tracks, Jesse took in the beauty that was Noel. She was naturally beautiful and didn't have to enhance her beauty with makeup, although he noticed she was wearing some that night. The red lips stick made her pouty lips appear fuller. Jesse took in a deep breath.

"You look...beautiful," Jesse's throat closed, and his mouth went dry.

"Thank you," Her body grew hot as if someone had doused her with fire.

"Oh Jess, I forgot to tell you. Noel here snagged a date with Jimmy Wren. Isn't that wonderful?" Sara asked sneaking up behind him. She snaked her arm through Jesse's all the while glaring at Noel. Her look said, *He's mine.*

Jesse's eyebrows shot up his forehead, "Jimmy Wren?" Jealousy punched the air from his lungs, it was all he could do not to react.

"I mean we haven't talked in ages and...he asked so..." Noel trailed off.

"And well, it's just perfect! Isn't it just perfect, Jess?" Sara raved.

"Yes, that sounds–nice. So, you won't be joining us for dinner then?" Jesse asked, disappointment tainting his voice.

"Not tonight, no." Noel shook her head, relieved that she didn't have to spend an awkward night with Jesse and Sara. "Well, I better be going, night," she said as she walked out of the room. Jesse's eyes following the girl until the door closed behind her back.

* * *

The rustic cabin towered before Noel. Beautiful yellow lights burned from each window, inviting her in. Butterflies flitted in her stomach. Was this a good idea? She'd be going home soon after all. Jana seemed to be getting stronger, but Noel wanted to spend this Christmas with the Wellings anyway. At the Wellings' age and how Jana's health had been, she may not get another chance to spend the holidays with them.

As she rose her hand to ring the doorbell, Jimmy swung the door open. "There you are! I thought I heard you pull–"

Noel didn't hear the rest of his words as she was knocked over backwards by something heavy, large, and furry.

"Ump," All the air in her lungs was expelled as she lay flat on her back. Milliseconds later, the fluffy beast bombarded Noel's face with extremely wet kisses.

"Gunner! Get back, you vile demon. Come on," Jimmy grabbed the large chocolate lab by its collar pulling him off of Noel.

Noel's laughter rang off the hills Jimmy's house was nestled in. "Oh my! What a handsome fella!"

She sat up to her knees and scratched the animal behind his ears. The chocolate-colored creature happily wagged his tail and stretched his neck

69

until he could gift her with a few more enthusiastic kisses.

"Sorry about that," Jimmy wrangled the dog back inside. "Come on in, make yourself comfortable. I'm just going to put him out back for a bit."

Chuckling, Noel dusted herself off and went inside. Jimmy's home was beautiful. The main room was huge and open., She fell in love with the vaulted ceilings. To the left a large cozy fire was crackling and to the right the kitchen housed a beautiful log table. The table was set complete with white lilies and candles that burned brightly.

"Well, that's not the welcome I'd planned for you." Jimmy's voice boomed from behind.

"Think nothing of it. I love animals." Noel smiled wondering if her hair was a complete mess after her greeting.

"Well, he's a rug rat for sure. If you believe it, he was being trained to be a service dog, but he was so hard-headed they couldn't do anything with him. The company who trained him was at their wits end so, long story short I got stuck with the scoundrel."

Noel laughed, trying to picture the tornado of a dog as a service animal. The massive amount of destruction that would ensue would be nothing short of a natural disaster.

Jimmy walked to the table and pulled out a seat for Noel. "Have a seat. I just pulled the steaks off the grill when you pulled up."

"Everything looks amazing," Noel took in the fresh salad, steaks, and baked potatoes he'd prepared.

"Can I offer you a drink?" Jimmy held up a bottle of wine.

Shaking her head, Noel held her hands up, "No, thanks. I don't drink….my dad made sure of that."

Jimmy's face reddened. "I'm so sorry, I completely forgot!"

"Don't worry about it, really. Ice water would be nice, and please don't hold back on my account."

"Ice water it is," Jimmy strolled to the kitchen. "To be honest I'm not much of a drinker now days. I ruined myself back in my wild years. Now I'd rather have a nice steaming cup of coffee over an import any day. So, how are your parents?" He asked loudly over the grinding of the ice maker.

"I don't know really. Dad took off years ago. The last time I saw mom was to bail her out of jail." Noel shrugged.

Jimmy said setting her ice water before her. "I hate you lived with that for so long."

"It wasn't so bad. I had the Wellings, and they made everything bearable. These steaks are incredible by the way. Where did you learn to cook?" Noel said between mouthfuls of melt-in-your-mouth steak.

She was getting spoiled to all the good cooking since coming back home. When she was by herself, which was almost always, she just stopped at a drive-through or tossed something in the microwave.

"That would be from my mom. I guess it was maybe our junior year she took some culinary classes at the community college."

"I remember that!" Noel smiled remember seeing his mother come into the pharmacy when she worked there during summer breaks. The single mom had been proud to wear her chef's uniform everywhere.

"Yeah, she decided Jared and I needed to learn to cook for ourselves and for our future wives. I'm glad she did because Jen couldn't cook to save her life." Jimmy smiled sadly thinking of his wife.

"Ah, the poor dear. I'm not much of a cook myself. Although I can order some mean Chinese." Noel said between bites.

"You're kidding? Jana Wellings never taught you any of her kitchen secrets? That's the only reason I asked you over! I need her secrets!" Jimmy smiled wickedly.

Noel threw her napkin at Jimmy's head. "You're awful you know that!"

"Yeah well," he shrugged tossing the napkin right back at her.

She laughed snagging the napkin in the air. "Just so you know Jana, shares her secrets with no one." Noel said. "But I suppose I never asked. She loved spoiling us kids and we loved being spoiled."

"That she did. There isn't a better soul around than Jana Wellings." Jimmy said thinking back on the years he, Jesse, and Noel would hang out at the Wellings house. Jana always had snacks waiting for them when they walked in the door. His own mother had been amazing but if he didn't have her he'd have loved to have Jana as a mother himself. In her own way, she was like a mother to them all.

Noel smiled, "No truer word has ever been spoken. However, right now I want to talk about something a little more important...something I think you've been avoiding."

Confusion and shock cover his beard face, "What? I don't know what you're talking...oh right," his grin traveled from ear to ear as he realized that she was referring to a video game they had played together as children. "You think you still got what it takes, cupcake? No matter what that little piece of paper says I am the reigning champ around these parts!"

Laughing, Noel said, "Bring it on buddy, but prepare to meet your demise!"

"Alright, but don't go crying when you get the Tetris beat down of your life, sweetheart! There isn't anyone here to save you now." Jimmy's face dropped into mock seriousness.

With a stern face, she narrowed her eyes on Jimmy. "Those are fighting words, kind sir!"

"You're darn right they are," Jimmy growled dropping his silverware playfully onto to table. "Head on into the living room. I have to let the beast in, so brave yourself. Also, I have to dig the game system out."

"Oh, don't go to any trouble, I was just kidding. I can't believe you kept that thing," Noel called.

"Backing out already?" Jimmy clucked like a chicken.

"Ha, not likely. I'm just giving you a chance to not get beat by the Tetris Champ of Old Harmony."

Jimmy walked back in the room. The small dusty box looked tiny in his massive hands. "I told you I was sick that day," he whined. Laughing so hard tears leaked from her eyes, Noel remembered the day well.

It was the end of their junior year and the PTO had put together a video game night for the upcoming seniors. Noel signed up for the Tetris competition. She played that game for hours beating opponent after opponent. Jesse had been beat early on, and he sulked in the corner over his failure. It came down to her and Jimmy.

Jimmy had unfortunately snuck a little spiked punch into the school event and had one too many cups. By the time he played Noel, she was on a roll and he was on his way to pukesville. It was a close match and Noel's stack of blocks climbed dangerously close to the top then…it happened. Red punch, pizza, and things unknown spewed from the depths of Jimmy's stomach that day.

Noel hung on ignoring the gut-retching sounds coming from Jimmy who sat next to her. Principle Turner smelled the alcohol as it erupted from the depths of Jimmy's stomach. Noel battled on as Jimmy's stack of cubes climbed higher and higher. As he was being drug off to the principal's office to call his mother, Noel did a little victory dance as she was crowned the Tetris Champ of Old Harmony High. Jimmy had been begging for a rematch since that day.

"Alright, Your Royal Highness, you ready to be dethroned?" Jimmy asked, handing her the remote and flopping next to her on the couch.

CHAPTER TWENTY-FOUR

Noel stumbled from her room, the overwhelming scent of coffee beckoned to her. Staying up past midnight was not a normal occurrence for her body and she was paying for it, but the night had been fun. She had forgotten how much fun it was to spend time with Jimmy. He was sweet, charming, funny, and it didn't hurt that he was easy on the eyes. She couldn't conceal the grin that came to her face when she thought about Jim.

"Good morning Miss Noel, how was your date? I hope it went better than dinner did here last night." Marta said raising her eyebrows at Noel's rough appearance.

"Last night was great actually–wait, what happened here?" Noel asked pouring a cup of freshly brewed coffee.

"I'm so glad you asked! It's that awful Sara Rhymes. She started in last night as soon as you left for your date. She just—"

"Not a date. Just two friends catching up." Noel interrupted.

"Hmph," Marta snorted. "ANY-ways, she was upset by Mr. Jesse's reaction when he saw you all dressed up, and rightly so I might add. That boys' tongue was hanging out looking at you," Marta jabbed.

"It was not!" Noel gasped trying not to laugh at the outspoken woman.

"And she took cheap shots at him about you all night. Finally, Mrs. Jana landed into her good. Unfortunately, it was too much for Mrs. W, and Mr.

W had to take Mrs. W to the hospital because her blood pressure skyrocketed."

Noel listened to the story with rapt attention, and the more Marta spoke the angrier Noel became. There was no amount of coffee that would make what she was hearing any better.

Clenching the coffee mug in her hand, Noel's blood boiled. "Where is she?"

"Mrs. W? She's back safe in her bed. Once she calmed down a bit her blood pressure–"

Noel raised her hand to silence Marta, "Not, Jana. Sara, where's she? Where does she live?"

"Oh no Miss Noel, you can't go there! Think of Mrs. W and what another blow-up could do to her. She's just now gaining back some strength." Marta placed her hand on Noel's wrist.

Mentally counting to five, Noel allowed her body to relax. "You're right…" Noel allowed a deep breath to leave her nose. "What good would come of that?"

"Exactly right," Marta continued talking a million miles a minute, but Noel blocked her out thinking only of the sweet woman who felt the need to defend her against the likes of Sara Rhymes. She may not confront Sara, but Jesse was a different story. Maybe it was time to check out Mr. Wellings' art gallery and see what all the fuss was about.

CHAPTER TWENTY-FIVE

The gallery was nothing like she expected. It was so much more. If she weren't so upset with Jesse and his choice of a mate, she would've admitted that the gallery was perfect. Jesse's work had always been amazing, but now after years of honing his skills, his work was brilliant, sharp, and beautiful.

The room had a very modern feel and was tastefully decorated in natural wood and muted shades of creams and grays. Three of the walls were adorned with paintings using different mediums. The front of the building was glass, and Jesse had displayed some beautiful pieces facing the outside. She briefly wondered if the sun would ruin them?

As she looked around, one piece made her stop in her tracks, and tears filled her eyes. The painting depicted a small boy and girl sitting under a large oak tree. The giant, twisted trunk covered in crackled bark was adorned with brightly colored leaves just before winter claimed them as its own. The rolling hills of their hometown filled the canvas, the grass in various shades of green, just before it gave into to its seasonal death.

He hadn't drawn faces on the children, but she knew who they were, the platinum blond girl and the dark haired, skinny boy. How many summers had she and Jesse sat under that tree sharing their hopes, dreams, and greatest fears?

"Thank you for coming to Wellin—oh Noel, what a pleasure." Sara said, her nose wrinkling as if a bad smell had invaded her senses.

"Is Jesse around?" Noel asked stiffening her back. She wasn't in the mood to deal with Sara. But she would if she had to.

"He's on a conference call. He's working with some buyers in China on some of his work." Sara held her head high, a possessive pride radiated from her being.

"Impressive. Can you let him know I'm here, and I'll wait as long as it takes." Noel raised her eyebrows challenging her rival. Her voice registered anything but impressed—although deep inside, she really was. China!

Sara studied Noel for a moment, a smug smile crossed her face, then asked. "How was your date?"

Noels nostrils flared, "It wasn't a date, but it went fantastic. Jimmy and I were good friends back in high school. At any rate, I assume my night went better than yours."

"Does he know that?" Sara asked choosing to ignore the dig about the night before.

"Of course, he knows that. Jimmy understands I'm here for Jana and John. Once Christmas break is over, I will be headed back home far, far away from here. It was just one dinner. No one in their right mind could imagine the night was anything more than two friends catching up."

Sara walked dangerously close to Noel. She glanced around the room then lowered her voice. "I want you to stay away from Jesse, you hear me?"

"Sara, honey, don't be fooled into believing I won't mow you down if you mess with me. I can be as sweet as they come, but don't test me. Believe me when I say if you hurt *my* family like you did last night, you'll wish your perfect, pampered, little butt had never met the likes of Jess–"

"Noel? Sara? What's going on?" Jesse asked coming from his office.

Sidestepping Sara, Noel zoned in on Jesse. "We need to talk, as soon as possible and preferably outside of your parents' home." Jerking her thumb toward Sara, Noel continued, "It'd be even better if *she* wasn't present!"

"What you have to say to me you can say in front of Sara," Jesse said gently. His heart pounded. Noel's face when she spoke to Sara was a scary sight. He wasn't certain what would have happened had he not come out when he did.

Sara stepped up to Jesse and planted her petite hand on his chest over his heart, "Jess, maybe you should talk to her alone." Fixing her doe-like eyes on him, she pouted slightly. "She just needs some attention, I think."

Sara and Jesse shared a knowing look at one another before Jesse agreed. Noel rolled her eyes watching as Jesse fell victim to the demon woman's ridiculous charm. "Yes, you're right."

Noel scrunched her eyes looking at the pair closely. The look they shared contained a hidden meaning. She had a feeling she was going to find out soon enough what that meaning was. She was afraid to move or speak, her anger once again rising. What kind of pull did this woman have over Jesse?

"Sure, how about Mel's?" He looked down at his watch. "Let's say in thirty minutes? I have a few more calls to make." Jesse looked from Sara to Noel. His wide-eye gaze was the look of a man stuck between two hungry lions. One wrong move, and he could lose his head.

"See you then," Noel stomped from the gallery. She trudged across the street to the pharmacy needing to vent to the one person she knew would understand.

CHAPTER TWENTY-SIX

Jimmy watched Noel plow across the square. Based on her rigid stance and the steam streaming from her ears, she'd just had it out with Jesse or Sara. Either way things didn't look good.

"Hey-" Jimmy plastered a smile across his face and hoped he wasn't about to catch her wrath. The woman looked ready to take on a raging bull.

"That...that-woman is...ugh!" Noel beat the side of her legs with her tiny fists.

Jimmy tapped his chin pretending to think. "Let me guess...do you speak of the pleasantly sweet Ms. Rhymes?"

"You know, I've tried being nice but...but," Noel sputtered.

"Janie, I'll be right back," Jimmy called over his shoulder, guiding Noel out of the store before she ran his customers off. "Come with me, let's go for a walk."

Reluctantly, Noel followed Jimmy outside. "The cool air's good for you, helps clear the mind."

"I can't go too far. I'm meeting Jesse at Mel's in about twenty minutes." Noel pulled her phone out to check the time.

"Perfect, I'll walk you there while you dish out all that Sara-hate on me."

Snorting Noel told Jimmy what Marta shared with her that morning. She shared every detail all the way to the passive-aggressive encounter she experienced with Sara in the gallery.

"Well, maybe you should talk with Jesse, but going in with guns a-blazing may not be the best approach. For some unknown reason, Jesse cares for Sara, and he may not take too kindly to a Sara showdown. But, you're right. He needs to hear it from an outsider, just be careful-you haven't been around for a long time. Jesse won't take kindly to being pushed around. There are old wounds that haven't healed when it comes to you and Jess."

Noel contemplated Jimmy's words, giving him a swat, she growled. "Dang it you're right. I'm just so angry, how can he let her talk and act that way to Jana and Pops? I mean Jana's...ill, and she's starving for attention from her son. I mean how did that happen? Jesse had always liked spending time with them before...now he's there once a week?"

She scraped the sleeve of her jacket across her eyes. The wind chilled her tear-streaked cheeks.

The pair walked in silence for a few more moments until they reached Mel's Diner. By then the tears freely flowed from Noel's eyes.

"Come here," Jimmy stopped and wrapped his arms around Noel. She rested her cheek against the soft wool of his jacket, reveling in his warmth. "It's okay, really. If anyone can get through to Jesse, it's you. Tell you what, how about I take you out for dinner tonight? There's a new Italian restaurant down in Mercer. I'll pick you up say...seven-ish and you can tell me how everything went?"

Nodding her head, Noel agreed. "That sounds good," she frowned still upset. "Thank you for being here for me." Standing on her tippy toes, Noel kissed Jimmy's cheek.

"Here comes Jesse," Jimmy backed away. "I'll see you at seven," he reminded her then strolled back towards the pharmacy.

Jesse approached, an awkward smile crossed his face when he passed Jimmy, "Let's go inside. Shew...it's cold."

The familiar voice, rough from years of heavy cigarette smoke called from the back. "Have a seat where you want!"

Mel Bradley, the owner of Mel's Diner. popped her head through the chef's window, "I'll be...a son of a monkey's uncle! Noel Miracle and Jesse Wellings-aren't you two a sight for sore for old eyes! Y'all grab you a seat! How about the regular if I can still remember it!"

Noel and Jesse both readily agreed. Every day after school during their high school years, Noel and Jesse would ride the bus to Wellings' pharmacy, beg Pops for food money, and then walk the few blocks to Mel's diner for a cheeseburger, extra pickles and ketchup, fries, and a strawberry shake with extra whipped cream and three cherries on top.

"Let's sit in the back," Jesse pointed to an empty booth in the back.

Noel smiled—their favorite booth. It was by the window, so they could people watch as they shared their days with one another. There was a baseboard heater that ran along the bottom of the wall keeping their feet warm during the winter.

"Jess," Noel started her heart softening just looking into his big, boyish eyes.

He held up his hand to silence her. "Please, let me start."

Sitting back, she spread her arms wide, "Go ahead."

"Sara's...concerned your presence...isn't good for my mother. She feels, maybe you should stay in a hotel and just come for short visits during the day."

Staring at Jesse as if he grew an extra head, Noel remained speechless. She should have popped Sara a good one when she had the chance.

"Mom and Pops need me more. I haven't been there for them like I should've been. Having you here and seeing how lonely she and Pops are made me realize that." Tears filled Jesse's eyes.

Poor guy, he was hurting, and she knew it broke his heart to hurt his parents, but she also knew his emotions were out of whack because of the Bride of Satan he kept in his life. She wanted to feel sorry for him, but she also wanted to pull him by his ears until he realized what he was saying.

"Do you hear yourself right now?" Noel asked in a hushed whisper. "I came here at the request of you and your parents. You mother wants me here."

"I know but maybe just for a little–" Jesse interjected. He looked confused as to why he was even having this conversation. Noel had to wonder if Sara was a puppet master controlling Jesse's every move.

"We don't have a little anything left when it comes to your parents. They are getting older, and their health is failing. Have you looked at Pops lately? He's stressed and worn down, and Momma Jay does look a little better, but they're getting older Jess."

"I know..." Jesse fiddled with the paper placemat that had a picture of Mel's face back in her younger glory days.

Noel continued, "What do *you* want me to do here Jesse? Leave? Break your mother's heart? I want to tell you I can walk away, but now that I'm back...I don't know that I can. Not until it's time for me to leave. We have a little over two weeks before I go back home. I think we can work this out until then."

"Sara–" he started again.

Her nostrils flared along with her temper, her voice raised almost to a shriek. "Sara can shove it up that tight little rear of hers. What happened to you Jess? Is she that special to you? Are you that blind? Or do all males just act like idiots when a pretty little thing with a tight body is around?"

He looked at Noel. Confusion filled his eyes. How could she say those things to him?

"Blind to what?" He asked, his eyebrows climbed up his forehead. She could see pink tint his cheeks. She knew they were traveling into dangerous waters, but she didn't care.

"She's jealous," Noel spat.

"Here we go, you two," Mel placed two large platters heaping with crispy, golden fries and a thick, juicy burger with all the trimmings.

"Thank you, Mel," Noel smiled at the woman.

Mel beamed a gray, denture-filled smile at the pair. "Man, seeing you two together again is like a gift from Father Time himself. So good! Holler if you need me," Mel reached over and gave Noel a side hug.

"Thank you, Mel," Noel squeezed her back. She hated that her reunion with Mel was tainted with ill feelings towards Jesse and his beloved Sara.

When Mel was out of earshot, Jesse narrowed his eyes on Noel and asked, "What do you think Sara is jealous of?" He picked his burger up and took a huge bite, smacking his lips loudly. She gritted her teeth. He knew she hated hearing him chew his food.

"Me, your mom, anyone who takes the attention away from her perfect, princess self!" Noel's voice grew louder still.

"Be fair here, you don't know her." Taking a large pull of his strawberry milkshake he looked at Noel with a cocky grin.

Oh, ho ho buddy, you're not cute right now, she thought.

Snorting, Noel said, "I don't have to know her Jess, I can see it. Everyone around you sees it. She's not a good person. She is hurting those around you. She wants what your talent can bring to her. Trips around the world, art exhibits to New York, dinners with established artists and business owners. She's no fool, of course. I suppose if I hadn't made it out of Old Harmony on my own then I'd try to find a meal ticket as well."

He didn't hear but a few words that she said. Putting down his burger, he looked at Noel and asked coldly, "You'd know all about hurting people, wouldn't you?"

Gaping at Jesse, it was a full ten seconds before she could speak, "What're you implying? That I hurt people?"

"You were my best friend and, in an instant," he snapped his fingers "you took that away from me. You just left. No goodbye, nothing. And now...now it's hard to even look at you. And if you don't care that you hurt me, what about mom and dad? You broke their hearts as well."

His words held such venom it stung, "This is a mistake. We can't go back. We can't be friends."

Rummaging around in her purse, Noel fished out enough cash for the meals and a sizable tip for Mel. Noel jumped to her feet. She had to get away. Her emotions had begun to spin out of control. "I'm staying with your parents until I go back home. However, I'll make it easy for you. In the evenings, after you get off work, come and go as you please. I'll leave, so it's not hard for you *to look at me*. There's plenty I can do to keep myself busy. We won't have to see each other at all."

Slapping the cash down on the counter, she continued, "Just so you know, you abandoned me way before I left this town, when you decided to betray me in front of all our peers. You broke my heart, Jesse Wellings, I loved you-I was in love with you."

"Mel! I'm stealing your dishes!" Noel yelled, shoving a handful of fries in her mouth.

Mel nodded and shrugged. She had been leaning over the counter listening to the entire exchange. She knew what was about to happen, either Jesse was going to wear a pink milkshake the rest of the day or Noel was gonna storm out. Mel didn't blame the kid. There was a lot of history between those two.

Turning on her heels, Noel walked out of the quaint diner, her back ramrod straight and her head held high and full of fries. She left before seeing the shock that registered across Jesse's face, and he missed the tears that streamed down hers.

Her anger carried her through the blistering cold straight to her car. Once inside the small sports car, Noel laid her head on her steering wheel and cried, cursing the day she had ever met Jesse Wellings.

CHAPTER TWENTY-SEVEN

How did that go south so quickly? Jesse asked himself staring at a framed poster of Elvis that towered before him. Mel loved Elvis and half her décor had something to do with The King.

All he wanted was peace, and he hadn't had than since his mom requested to have Noel as a house guest. Was that too much to ask for? Sara was behaving like a caged animal and Noel was just as stubborn as she'd always been. The two women were going to drive him insane.

Noel was being unreasonable, and he wanted to scream until his lungs collapsed. But he also had an undeniable urge to pull her into his arms and feel her soft, pink lips against his. A shiver danced down his spine as he shook the thought from his head.

More than anything however, he wanted to punch Jimmy Wren in the nose for getting her attention so easily. How had that happened so quickly? The young pharmacist with his rugged good looks, fancy home, and just...everything!

Rage filled his being as he thought about how nicely Noel fit in Jimmy's embrace. A burning hot anger broiled deep inside his gut as he thought of Noel planting her full, pouty lips against his cheek. The pair looked so cozy all snuggled up with one another, right there in public too!

"You okay kid?" Mel slid in the booth across from him looking at his half-filled plate.

"I... yeah, sorry about that," he jerked his thumb over his shoulder. He rubbed his hands over his eyes, a headache was forming.

"Ya kiddin'? I'm glad ta see tha two of you back togatha," Mel's thick country accent made him smile.

"I don't know if she feels the same," he sighed.

"Have ya told 'er you love 'er yet? Or are ya still running with that uppity little…" her voice trailed off, but Jesse got her meaning. He ignored Mel's comment. She was an old country gal who spoke her mind, and to her, most women were uppity little something or others.

"Love Noel? No…we were just good friends…once upon a time anyways." Jesse cleared his throat and looked around the room nervously. Why is Mel up in his business, and why was he participating in the conversation?

"Hmmm, I guess if you won't make your move that large, handsome hunk of a man Jimmy Wren sure will. What I wouldn't do for one hot evening with that lug–"

"Mel!" Jesse interrupted, not wanting to hear what the old woman would do with Jimmy Wren.

"Oh sorry," Mel cackled. "Forgive me it's been a while since Marty passed." She sighed, "A woman's gotta dream, don't she?" Mel raised her eyebrows up and down at him. She slid back out of the booth as Jesse shifted awkwardly in the plastic covered seat. The old woman laughed.

She stopped and leaned over just so Jesse could hear her, "Better figure out what ya really want son. That Jimmy's a mover. He'll sweep that girl off her feet in a hot minute. Not that he's not a catch…just saying I'd love to see the two of you togatha is all, but maybe I'm just an old romantic."

"Um, thanks?" Jesse was at a loss for words.

"Don't be a stranger now. Even big-shot artists need to eat some good old southern cooking every now and again. An clean that plate before ya leave now, ya hear?" Then she walked off humming the tune of *You Ain't Nothin' but a Hound Dog.*

CHAPTER TWENTY-EIGHT

The restaurant was quaint, quiet, and romantic. Noel admired the stone walls, high archways, and eclectic collection of art that ranged from replicas of famous sculptures to very nice copies of famous works from Italian artists. The atmosphere was peaceful, and the candle-lit tables were a nice touch to the carefully decorated facility…a little slice of Italy in an unlikely country town.

How long had it been since someone had taken her somewhere so nice? The guys she dated thought a night out for pizza and beer was a five-star event. Not that a good slice of pizza wasn't amazing, but every now and then being pampered with a nice dinner out and good conversation was amazing.

"This place is nice for Mercer. Although I must say, the town has grown since I was home last." Noel took in the serene vibe of the Italian bistro.

Jimmy smiled, "Yeah, there're some pretty neat places popping up in this town. If only progress would spread to Old Harmony we'd be set."

"I don't know. I'm afraid Old Harmony would lose its small town charm." Noel said running her fingers along the silky, white table cloth that covered their table.

"Maybe," Jimmy agreed twirling the last of his spaghetti on his fork. "From a business owner's standpoint, I like not having much competition in town, but a few five-star restaurants would be nice."

Noel sighed, "I can't argue there. Mel's is nice, but Roxy's Bistro is top notch. I can barely breathe I ate so much."

He chuckled. She certainly ate more than he thought her small frame could hold. "Me too, I've come here at least once a week since they opened but never with such beautiful company."

"At least you don't mind seeing me," she mumbled thinking of Jesse.

Jimmy sighed, pushing his empty dish away. "Take it easy on Jesse. He's going through a lot."

"Gah, I mean, I know but how can he let that vile woman tell him how to live his life? I'm no threat to her. Once winter break is over, I'll head home and likely not return for a good long while." Noel fumed.

"I hate to hear that," Jimmy said looking at Noel, his big brown eyes intense. "You know, I was talking to Joyce Spencer, and she said they had several openings at the elementary school here in Mercer—you could come back home."

"Thanks, I'll think about it, but after my conversation with Jesse, I'm not sure there's much left here for me." Noel admitted.

"You have more than you think. Right now it's easier for Jesse if he hides behind Sara and lets her make stupid decisions for a while. I mean Jesse's a great guy, but other than having you around, he was an only child. Think of how awful it must be to know the people who brought you up...are not always going to be around. They don't have any other family, and I'm sure he's just scrambling to hold onto something, and that something is Sara right now."

"You're right, I need to get over it, but he makes me so mad. Like, it wouldn't have even bothered me had I believed he really wanted me to stay away but it's her!" Noel vented.

"I get you. Sara Rhymes is trouble. She always has been. Right now, Jesse has fallen victim to her charm." Jimmy shared Noel's sentiments when it came to Sara Rhymes.

"I hope he gets wise to her ways, but enough about Jesse. What I need to know is when do I get my rematch?" Noel changed the subject. She realized she was being rude talking of Jesse while out with Jimmy. He was good-natured about it, but all the same, it was rude.

Chuckling Jimmy asked, "You've already been dethroned princess. Are you sure you're ready to be humiliated again?"

Opening her mouth in righteous indignation, Noel whined, "Your dog attacked me!"

Jimmy roared with laughter, "He wanted some affection!"

"Affection my foot! When a hundred pounds of brown fluff jumps on your lap and licks your face nearly off your head during a one-on-one grudge match-one knows his master put him up to it!" Noel said wagging her finger at her date.

Wiping his eyes with the back of his hand, Jimmy replied, "Don't blame Gunner, lady, you finally met your match!"

"Who, you or Gunner?" Noel shot back. "You told that dog to jump on me, didn't you?"

Jimmy didn't answer but his eyes danced with mischievousness as he waged his eyebrows.

"Confess mister," she demanded.

Still laughing, Jimmy gave in. "Alright, I may have given him the signal, but the rest was all him. It's not my fault if he sees you as an irresistible snack!"

Noel raised her chin in mock astonishment, "Well, I never!"

After a few chuckles, Jimmy grew serious. "So, um," he cleared his throat. "The Tree Lighting Festival is this Saturday evening, and I'd love it if you'd accompany me."

Noel looked down at her hands suddenly shy. Jimmy was so handsome, fun to be around, and a true gentleman. He was incredible really, but a pang of guilt hit her stomach. Jesse was the one who stayed on her mind.

Jesse has Sara, she reminded herself.

She looked up and smiled sweetly, "It's been years since I've been! I'd love to go with you!"

The tree lighting festival was her favorite. Almost everyone in town showed up in the town square for hot cocoa, apple cider, or eggnog. It was a nice event as folks mingled with one another. The kids received a visit from Santa, and the adults participated in a huge snowball fight. If it hadn't yet snowed, the city brought in a snow machine and made the downtown area a winter wonderland for the townspeople.

All the businesses closed early, but the business owners all did something special for the event. There was a sense of community within the town. When they were younger, Jana and Pops set up a booth and handed out a steaming mug of Momma Jay's famous hot coco and chocolate chip cookies. The hardware store handed out bags of miniature candy canes, and a few of the boutiques gave away sweet little keepsakes that always had something to do with Kentucky or Old Harmony itself.

The local Baptist church and the gospel choir took turns singing traditional and some non-traditional Christmas carols. The evening was full of love, music, and Christmas spirit. Noel sighed. She needed a bit of Christmas Spirit this year. Jesse and Sara had her so wound up she hadn't thought much about the holiday other than wishing it were over.

"I have to work later that evening so how about you come up and meet me at the pharmacy around seven-thirty?" Jimmy broke through her thoughts.

"That sounds perfect! Now let's get back to you and that cheating dog of yours." She poked.

CHAPTER TWENTY-NINE

Once again Noel spent a great deal of time preparing for her date. It was nice to dress up, and she wanted to look nice in case she ran into old friends from high school. She shouldn't care what they thought of her at this point, but she did. The Tree Lighting Festival was always a semi-dressy affair for the adults anyways.

"Oh dear, you look lovely! I suppose you'll be meeting a certain tall, handsome, bearded man for the Tree Lighting Festival?" Jana asked, her pale face a sickly green.

"He did ask me to accompany him," Noel nodded shyly. Looking at Jana however, she wondered if she shouldn't stay back with her.

"You look absolutely stunning! That Jimmy Wren is one lucky man," Jana boasted. Her pride for the girl she loved bloomed in her chest. She couldn't have loved the child anymore if she were her own.

"I'm lucky to have a friend like him, especially since…"

Jana's face wrinkled in disgust, and she leaned over in a conspiratorial whisper said, "Since that Sara Rhymes cast her spell over our Jesse? Yes, I agree but I know my son, this mess with Sara won't stick. He's just lost and confused and when someone feels helpless they cling to those that have it all together. Right now, Sara's taking care of the things that Jess can't because he's hurting over my illness."

"I'm sure you're right. She sees me as a threat, and I don't know why!" Noel grumbled.

"Sounds like Jesse isn't the only dense one in this situation," Jana clucked her tongue.

"Wha–" Noel gasped. Did Momma Jay just call her dense?

"Don't act surprised little lady, I know you as well as I know my son. And you my sweet girl have loved that boy long before you knew what true love was. That's why whatever tiff you two had still stings as it does." Jana added gently.

"Even if you're right, Jesse never felt that way about me. I was like his kid sister. And now with Sara in his life, I'll likely not even be that."

"Hmm, I would've agreed with you had I not seen the gleam in his eye when you mentioned a date with Jimmy. I believe there are somethings you don't fully understand about Jesse. Hopefully one day you two will get a chance to get some things out in the open." Jana spoke wisely.

"Do you really think so?" Noel asked skeptically.

"As sure as I know you're going to be late for the festival if you don't stop yammering here with me and leave right now." Jana reminded the girl it was time to go.

"Oh, shoot you're right." Bending to kiss the woman's hollowed cheek, Noel left in a flurry of hugs, kisses, and a quick goodbye to Marta.

*   *   *

The pharmacy was closed by the time Noel made it to town, but Jimmy was waiting out front for her. "Sorry, I was running late!" Noel called hopping out of her car.

"It's fine. I just closed up, shall we?" He offered his arm to Noel. She hooked her arm through his.

"Oh, look it's starting to snow!" Noel said. The city had already rented the snow machine and downtown looked like a winter wonderland, but there was nothing like a true snow fall to set the mood.

"It's nice," Jimmy looked down at her his eyes taking in her beauty. "You look breathtaking tonight."

She had chosen a loose red knit sweater, custom fit jeans, and a charcoal pea coat for the evening. She topped it with a vintage 1920's red flapper hat she'd picked up at a thrift shop months ago. With her platinum hair fixed in shiny waves she looked as if she belonged to a different time.

92

The cool air turned her pale cheeks a beautiful shade of blush, and the moon glistened in her gray eyes. She glowed under his praise.

"You clean up pretty nice yourself, sir," she replied looking him over. She'd never figure out how that man could make a plaid flannel shirt look sexy, but he did. There was a rugged, handsomeness to Jimmy that was hard to find.

"How was your day?" He asked.

She smiled. It was nice to be asked how her day was. How long had it been since anyone had cared?

"It was nice. I spent some quality time with Jana this afternoon. It's hard seeing her so sick but the closer to Christmas we get, the happier she seems."

"That woman *is* Christmas. I truly believe she was sent from above just to show the rest of us commoners how to do the holiday right."

She chuckled, "You're not wrong. She brought magic into my life year-round, but Christmas was always special when I was with Jana. Oh Jim, look!"

Noel pointed to the crowd of people gathered around the large pine tree that towered in the center of town square. Jimmy smiled at the childlike way her eyes lit up and the cheer of happiness that left her lips.

The Tree Lighting Ceremony had come a long way in the years since she'd been gone. Strands of brightly colored lights ran from one side of the street to the other. Mini Christmas trees stood proud at each corner. *How had I missed seeing this?* She asked herself. She knew how…thoughts of a handsome lumberjack and a serious artist clouded her mind.

The tree had to be thirty-foot-tall, and hundreds of red, gold, and silver baubles hung from its piney branches. A golden star adorned the top, watching over the townspeople. For the time being, the tree was the only inanimate object not doused in bright flickering Christmas lights.

"Yeah, a few years back, the town voted to use more funds to create a more memorable experience." Jimmy explained.

"Well, whoever's in charge of this does an amazing job," Noel said in awe allowing her senses to take over.

The gospel choir was up and singing their soulful version of Jingle Bell Rock that had the whole town swaying back and forth. The scent of sweet, sugar-roasted nuts and hot coffee filled her nostrils, her belly growled as she took in the scents. Unfortunately, there was no scent of Momma Jay's homemade chocolate chip cookies. A wave of sadness rolled over Noel. She wished she'd come home more to appreciate those sweet little things.

"That's quite a compliment coming from a big city girl like yourself, Noel Miracle." Cassandra said from behind. "And I suppose I should say, on behalf of the city council as their director, thank you!"

"Oh, you did this?" Noel asked. Noel drew her lips tight and grimaced, realizing she was being rude.

Cassandra laughed and gave a little bow. "Well, I had a great deal of help, but the Tree Lighting Festival is my baby."

Noel looked at the girl who had caused her such grief in high school. She'd been lazy, self-righteous, and mean. *Was she still that same person?* Noel wondered.

Laughing again, Cassandra said, "I can see what you're thinking, Noel. Yes, I was a snobby brat when we were kids, but things change, girl! I have to go now. The mayor will be looking for me, but I'm still waiting for that get together, so we can catch up."

Winking at Jimmy and patting Noel's hand, Cassandra pranced away, stopping every few feet to speak to the residents of Old Harmony.

Noel sighed. "How do I end up running into her everywhere I go?"

"Cassandra? She's not so bad, a few years back, she got mugged right here on the square by some out-of-towners and that experience changed her. She's a lot nicer, and she pushes for better laws and law enforcement to protect all of us. She even spent weeks going around the county hunting down people she had hurt in the past to apologize for how she acted when she was younger. I'm sure she wants to do the same for you."

"That's admirable, but it's hard to imagine you know? She tormented me all through high school, all the while making me believe we were friends, but people do change."

"She was good at that," he nodded. "Don't look now, but a little more unpleasantness is strolling our way."

Looking up, Noel saw Jesse being pulled along, most reluctantly, by a gorgeous Sara Rhymes. "Lord help me," Noel muttered.

"Oh, Jess look! Here's Noel and Jimmy. It's so nice to see you two here." Sara wrapped Jesse's arm around her waist and laid her head on his shoulder. Noel barely concealed the snicker that forced its way through her nose. *I get it girl, he's yours,* Noel thought to herself.

"Hey guys," Jesse smiled, his eyes narrowed on Noel. "We're just headed to get something to drink."

"Join us," Sara's eyes lit up. Whatever she had planned, Noel wanted no part in it. Her eyes grew wide, and she looked to Jimmy for help.

"Oh, man we'd love to, but we were just headed out. I set up a surprise for Noel. Maybe next time, eh?" Jimmy shrugged and smiled good-naturedly.

"Yeah, next time," Jesse mumbled. He glared at Jimmy, despising how close the man was to Noel. Before Jimmy's sudden fascination with Noel, Jess had liked the guy. Now he wanted to power drive the man through a pile of snow. He also knew that he weighed half of what the massive man before him weighed and would likely bounce off.

"See ya later," Noel said avoiding Jesse's glare.

As the couple strolled away, Noel asked, "A surprise? Nice cover." She gave him a chummy jab in the side.

"Ouch, Wonder Woman, I think you broke a rib," he kidded nervously.

His heart thumped a little harder. Jimmy looked down at Noel. He hoped it wasn't too much. He didn't want to scare her off, but he had little time left to see if there was something real between them before she left town.

"Oh hush!" she bumped him with her hip.

"Anyway, it's true. I do have a surprise for you. Come with me," he said as he gently pulled her along beside him.

"What? Where're we going?" Noel laughed, trying to keep up with Jimmy's long strides.

"It's a surprise, sheesh." Jimmy rolled his eyes in mock annoyance. He did slow down a little as they reached the far end of the square.

"Here we are," Jimmy pulled out a set of keys and started to fumble around.

"The hardware store?" Noel giggled nervously. That side of the square was quiet. None of the festivities had made it to that little corner.

"You'll see," Jimmy said unlocking the door. "Come on in. Watch your step though. Straight back to the left."

"It's so dark," she giggled anxiously.

"Let me lock this door back so we don't have any unsuspecting party crashers. Here," he said, making his way towards her using his cell as a flashlight. "Through that door."

The metal door he pointed his light at lead to a set of stairs that went to the attic. "Where're you taking us, and how did you get the keys to the store? You're not some Christmas killer, are you?"

"You'll see," Jimmy snorted. At the top of the stairs was a storage room filled with boxes and cans of paint. To the back of the room was another door. "After you." Jimmy opened the door and stepped back, allowing Noel to exit first.

When her eyes adjusted to the area, her jaw dropped. Jimmy had set up a canopy and underneath was a tiny round table with candles and white Christmas lights strung overhead. There was a food warmer on the table and a thermos.

"Oh, it's so sweet! Did you do this?" Noel asked tears springing to her eyes.

"Yeah, I wanted to do something special for you. I know you've been having a hard time since you got back into town and well…" Nervously, he rubbed his hand on the back of his neck and looked away.

"No one has ever been this good to me. Thank you, Jimmy. You are such a special man."

Jimmy took a step close to Noel and looked into her eyes, the Christmas lights glimmering in them. "You're special to me, too," he said, his voice soft and sweet.

He leaned close. She could feel his breath on her cheek. Her heart thudded–this was happening. Someone like Jimmy wanted her. Slowly she leaned in, ready to meet his mouth to hers. Closing her eyes, she was just millimeters away.

Just a breath away, and she pulled back. She needed to breathe, she needed space, why did she move away? Jimmy was as close to perfect as she'd ever dated. *He wasn't Jesse*, her brain reminded her.

"Look you can see the festival from up here!" Noel backed away from him, turning her interest to the town below.

Jimmy, reading her body language loud and clear, backed off but didn't show his disappointment. Instead, he pretended nothing had happened and decided that maybe all they'd ever be was friends. He could live with that if he had to. Noel Miracle was amazing enough that he could settle for just her friendship.

"Best seats anywhere. They should be lighting the tree soon. How about some hot chocolate? I brought a thermos up earlier." Jimmy grabbed the thermos and waved it in the air.

"That sounds lovely, "Noel said glad the tense moment between her and Jimmy wouldn't get in the way of their night.

"Here you go," he handed her a steaming cup of cocoa.

"Mm, this…" She took another sip. "Oh my, this tastes familiar, but how? She gives her recipes to no one." Noel's eyes grew wide, although it had been a few years. She knew the distinct flavors of Jana's homemade cocoa.

"She still won't part with her recipe., She made this herself and had John hand-deliver it to me at the pharmacy just minutes before you showed up. Yeah, I got pull with the Lady of Christmas like that," Jimmy swaggered.

Noel smiled at his silliness as well as the touching gesture from Jana. "That's why she looked so tired. She wore herself out to give me this?"

"I tried to ask her not to go to the trouble, but she's–" Jimmy started.

"Stubborn," The pair finished at the same time.

"That woman loves you, the whole family does…I miss having family around," Jimmy walked to the edge of the building he peered down to watch the families huddle close to one another to keep warm. Santa had just arrived, and droves of children flocked him at once.

"I'm sorry Jimmy, I can't imagine…" He was alone. His parents were both gone now, and his wife too had passed.

"I'm glad you have the Wellings." He said, not wanting to talk of his personal loss.

"I am too. They saved me from what the west side of town and my parents had planned. I never fully understood what living in those conditions could do to a child until I became a teacher." Noel thanked God, not for the first time, that He saved her from a life of pure torture when He put the Wellings in her life.

His eyes sought hers, "I bet you're an amazing teacher."

"Yeah, I'm kind of a big deal," she said with a little spice.

"Oh great, give you one complement and look what happens!" Jimmy chuckled.

Noel laughed giving his arm a playful shove. "Oh stop!"

"Listen, I think the mayor's about to light the tree…" Jimmy cocked his head to one side. The chatter below had died down and the hum of a speaker system buzzed through the crowd. "Yeah, there he is."

Jimmy wrapped his massive bicep around Noel's shoulders. He was so warm. Noel snuggled close to him. *What were they doing?* She asked herself.

She felt warm, safe, and comfortable with Jimmy, but the thought of more than a warm embrace made her want to head for the hills.

The mayor, with Cassandra by his side, spoke briefly about Christmas and family, giving the crowd a warm, fuzzy feeling. Minutes later he passed a giant gray box to Cassandra, who ceremoniously pressed a large red button on the box. Immediately, the tree illuminated the square. The brightly-lit tree cast flecks of light and sparkles across the entire downtown area. The lights cast lovely hues of reds and greens across the snow-covered ground.

"Say what you will about Cassandra, but the girl knows how create an amazing festival." Jimmy said.

"Yeah," she said in awe. "She does."

Noel looked up at his handsome face and watched him as he took in the beauty of the lights. Not for the time, she asked herself if all those feelings she harbored for Jesse should stay in the past, so she could have a life with someone like Jimmy.

CHAPTER THIRTY

Sneaking in the house at six am, Noel tiptoed through the back door. The home was deathly quiet and completely dark. Marta hadn't started her work for the day. Noel was grateful for Marta's absence as she wanted more than anything to snuggle into her bed and sleep for just a few more hours.

Creeping through the sitting room she had almost made it to the hallway leading to the bedrooms when a voice spoke from the depths of the room, "Pull an all-nighter?"

Jesse. "My God! You nearly scared me to death!" Noel scolded, the rapid drumming of her heart pounded against her chest.

Waiting for her eyes to adjust, she made out his silhouette sitting in his mother's easy chair.

"Want to talk about scared? I've been waiting here all night to make sure you made it home okay. Sara left hours ago, before the roads got bad. Where've you been?"

Jesse stood up and paced the floor, "I was about to call the cops and have them search for you."

"Well, I'm fine I just-" Noel began to explain.

"I called your phone a hundred times at least!" Jesse's voice clipped.

"It was dead Jesse. I forgot to put my charger back in my car before I left. After the festival I went back to Jimmy's to watch a movie, and we fell asleep. He drove me home on his way to work because Mountain Road was completely covered. My car wouldn't make it home."

"Yeah,,,watched a movie," Jesse said shooting her a deadly look his nostrils flaring.

Noel stomped her feet and took three large strides, standing before Jesse. Standing on her toes she pointed her finger in his face.

"Jesse Wellings, how dare you insinuate such a thing about me. Jimmy and I are just friends, but if we weren't that'd be none of your concern. You got that? You lost the privilege of giving me advice the day you chose impressing those idiots at school over defending me. Yes, I should be over it, but I can't move past how easy it was for you to dismiss me. If I'd been in your shoes, I would've boxed the ears of anyone who dared to disrespect you. I. Loved. You. With everything I had in me, I loved you. You were my—"

Without warning Jesse grabbed both sides of her face and pulled her to him. Passionately, he pressed his mouth to hers. It felt like an eternity, and it felt like seconds when he finally pulled away. She gasped at the intense emotions that burst through her mind, body, and soul at his touch. What had they done? Her heart flitted in her chest, she opened her mouth to protest but did she want to?

The pair stayed in shocked silence for several seconds, Jesse staring a hole through her and Noel with her mouth hinged open stupidly.. The pair stayed that way until the chipper voice of Marta billowed from behind, "Far be it from me to interfere with true love Mr. Jesse, but Miss Sara is pulling in the drive right now, and I'd say she wouldn't be too happy to find you in an..um…compromised position."

Jesse's face dropped in shock. "I'm sorry, I shouldn't have done that. I was just so relieved—that you were okay." He explained.

"Yeah, I know…it was…relieved, yeah. Listen I need to shower…ah…see you later." She pulled away from him, their faces dropped dumbly, surprised they were still wrapped in each others' arms.

Abruptly he let her go, "Sorry." He wiped his sweaty palms on his jeans.

"I…it's, it's okay," she said her face lighting up like a Christmas tree.

"Will you be here tonight?" He asked not wanting to leave her. He wanted to stay there and wrap her back in his arms and stay there forever.

"Jimmy asked…dinner—" the dryness of her throat prevented her words from coming out.

"Oh, sure of course. Well, another time." Jesse said backing away unable to tear his eyes from Noel.

Marta smiled at the two stammering fools. "Mr. Jesse…" she said in a sing song voice. "You should get going before the thing of evil comes to find you."

"Right, well," ignoring Marta's words about his girlfriend, Jesse patted Noel's shoulder awkwardly. "See you…"

"Yeah, see you." Noel said touching her fingers to her lips.

Stuck in the place where Jesse left her, Noel stood transfixed until Marta the eloquent spoke again. "Well, that's not what I meant by talking to the lad but that'll do Ms. Noel, that'll do."

"I'm taking a shower," Noel bolted from the room needing very much to be alone.

"A long cold one might do the trick Ms. Noel," Marta's words followed her down the hall.

*   *   *

Sleepily, Noel read a chapter of Great Expectations. Jana's eyes closed, Noel dropped the book to her lap and closed her own eyes as well. *Just for a second*, she thought.

"You going to stick around for dinner tonight dear?" Jana asked her voice thick with sleep.

Noel's eyes popped open quickly. "Um, Jimmy asked me out again tonight."

"Oh? Something fun I hope?" Jana tried to be excited, but her eyes drooped, and her head nodded.

"No… I mean, yes, just a quiet evening at his house. I think we are going to watch a sappy Christmas movie and eat popcorn."

"Well maybe you'll make it home before dawn this time?" Jana jabbed a twinkle in her eye.

"How did you–" Noel started.

Jana concealed an all-knowing smile, "I know everything that goes on in my home…mostly due to Marta and her insistent jabbering. However, there's one thing she wouldn't tell me…something to do with you and my son."

"Dang it Marta," Noel whispered. Jana's hairless brow lifted her forehead. "Want to enlighten me?" She asked suddenly more alert.

Sighing heavily, "I do but...its awkward, ya know?"

"I imagine it is," Jana smiled. "But you can try!"

"He kissed me, and I kissed him back. But it's not what I thought it'd be and so much more all at the same time."

"Oh?" Jana tiled her head to the side confused.

"I mean being close to him like that sent my brain reeling, but there's Jimmy and Sara and all this stuff from the past. I think it was poor timing. Maybe it always will be when it comes to Jesse and me." Noel sighed looking down at her hands.

"Maybe so, you two have a lot to figure out." Jana consoled the girl.

"Everything's so confusing, and I'm not here for that. To be honest, as sweet as Jimmy is I wouldn't be with him so much if it weren't for Sara coming around all the time. Don't get me wrong. Jimmy is so sweet, thoughtful, and amazing, but I don't plan on staying here forever. Old Harmony doesn't have much for me here anymore."

Jana grabbed Noel's youthful hand in her wrinkled, veiny one. "Don't put so much pressure on yourself. The good Lord will reveal all to you in due time. And one doesn't need much of a town except the people who love them."

Noel looked away from Momma Jay. She was right. There may not have been much in Old Harmony for her but there was even less where she lived currently. She had her job and the sweet kids she taught, but that was it. Truly she received more love from the Wellings than any other people she knew. Having Jimmy as a buddy was nice also. She had become so secluded since she left.

"You're right, you always are, but maybe I do have more here than I thought." Noel agreed giving Jana a big hug.

Jana yawned big, "Oh me! I'm so worn out, love. I think it's time for another nap. Stop in and see me before bed, if you make it back before sun up."

Noel chuckled. "I will, sleep well. I love you."

Noel bent over and kissed the woman's cool cheek. She felt better than she had earlier. Talks with Jana always left her feeling better–light, and nearly burden free. This is what she missed, having a mother figure there to lean on when life got rough. Guilt hit her in the gut. *Did Jana think she was awful for saying she had nothing in Old Harmony?* Under this very roof held a wealth of love that many people would never experience.

An overwhelming fear of never seeing Jana's sweet face, never receiving those words of wisdom squeezed her chest. *What was she doing?* She was wasting time running with Jimmy and fantasizing over Jesse, while the person who meant the most to her in the world could have died, and she'd have missed so much time with her. She had to get her life straight, starting tonight.

CHAPTER THIRTY-ONE

"Wow, you sure know your way around a kitchen!" Noel said sitting back in her chair, allowing her food to settle. She ate way too much and now her stomach was ready to explode.

"It's nice to have someone to cook for again," his words reminded Noel that she needed to have a tough conversation with Jimmy. "I've enjoyed having you around. I'll miss you when you leave. You better come visit more often than every six years, young lady!"

He pointed a spatula at her as he packed away the leftovers. She wished things were different, that her heart wanted him for more than just friendship. *Dang you Jesse Wellings*, she thought, *why can't you get out of my head.*

"Hey, why do you look so…poopy? Jimmy asked, cautiously.

Noel chewed the inside of her cheek for a moment thinking of how to answer him. "I'm going to miss you too. Break will be over sooner than I want it to. Jana seems weak still, but I think she'll be okay." Noel said.

Jimmy hesitated.

"What? Do you know something?" Noel asked her heart hammered in her chest.

"No, she should be fine. It's just that she still needs surgery, and they haven't cleared her for that yet. If she can make it until then she should be fine, it's just…" Jimmy didn't want to scare Noel but if Jana's doctors considered her too high of a risk for surgery she may never fully recover.

"She seemed so…" But it hit her, the almost transparency of Jana's skin, how even sitting up in bed seems to be a chore. Even the days when she had enough energy to get out of bed were few and she didn't last long before she needed to rest. What else was she missing while she was off enjoying herself with Jimmy?

"Jimmy, I think maybe I should–"

He finished her sentence for her, "Spend more time with the Wellings and less with me?"

She looked up and held his stare. There was no accusation from Jimmy, but complete understanding. Once again, she wished that Jesse Wellings would leave her mind. Adding patient, compassionate, and understanding to the *how Jimmy is wonderful list* Noel mentally kicked her own rump.

"Yes, I'm sorry this has been wonderful, but I need to be with them. They're my family."

Jimmy smiled sadly, "I know. Believe me when I say spend time with your loved ones while you can. You just never know…"

Noel stood and gave Jimmy a hug, "I'm sorry for what happened to you and to Jennifer."

"It was my fault really," He started, the words choking off in his throat. He had never shared with anyone what really happened the night his wife passed away.

"Don't blame yourself, we can't help these things." She tried to console. He pulled away and instantly Noel could see he needed to unload some serious junk, and it was major.

"She'd been running from me. I scared her," Noels heart leapt to her throat. *What had he done?*

"Why?" She whispered.

"I was stupid. You know how dumb I've always been. We were young, and I still acted quite foolish at times. One night I went out with the guys to watch a football game and had one too many drinks. I can't even remember who was playing. To be honest, I don't even remember driving home. She was upset because I missed dinner, she had tried too hard," his voice broke but he held it together. "God, I was so stupid. I yelled at her and threw some stuff around. You know–trying to deflect her accusations of my drinking problem. I went too far, and she had enough of my mouth and she took off scared."

He broke off for a moment reliving that terrible night all over again. "It'd been raining for hours that night and you know…the roads can be bad here…I thought I heard something—a loud crunching noise, but I brushed it off and went to bed. I thought she'd come back once she'd cooled off. Just a few hours later, I was woken up by the sheriff pounding on the door. It was too late. She was gone."

"Oh Jim," Noel wrapped her hand around her neck.

"She wrapped her car around a tree no more than a quarter mile from here. She stayed there for hours until one of the salt trucks came by and noticed her car turned over…while I slept off the booze." He still fought off the tears that filled his eyes.

"Jimmy, I'm so, so sorry. We all do crazy things, and I believe if Jennifer was anything like she was back in school, she wouldn't want you to hold all this in and beat yourself up. You're a great guy, and I'm sure she loved you a lot. I can't imagine her not loving you back."

"Spending time with you has lessened the pain a little, but I know the Wellings need you. And until you and Jesse figure out what's going on between you two, I have a feeling you won't be able to be serious with anyone, huh?"

Pulling away, Noel looked in Jimmy's eyes. He deserved her honesty. "I think you might be right," Noel looked deep into his eyes, her grey eyes growing large and serious. "But for now, I need you to get ready for a night of some of the sappiest, most romantic, Christmas movies to ever hit the screen."

"Fine," he rolled his eyes. "Go put one on, and I'll make some popcorn and drinks you crazy woman. You know, it's a good thing you won't date me. I could never be with a woman who revels in the worst movies known to man. Now get!" He playfully snapped a dish towel at her legs.

Squealing, Noel streaked into the living room, Gunner barking wildly at her heels. Jimmy's laughter followed her out of the room.

CHAPTER THIRTY-TWO

The house was dark and appeared as if everyone was already asleep. Noel looked at her phone. It was only ten-thirty, but the Wellings had always been "early to bed and early to rise" kind of people. She'd spend some time with Jana in the morning.

The lamp on her bedside table was lit for her, and her bed was turned down. It was nice to be cared for. Little things like a turned down bed meant so much. She was sure that for now, Marta was the one doing the work, but all the same she appreciated how they thought of her.

A pang of guilt filled her stomach thinking of how much they cared and how callously she'd left them. Calls home were infrequent. Many times, when she came to town to bail her mother out of jail she'd breeze in and out of town without letting them know. As wise and well-connected as Jana was, she likely knew that Noel had been around. *Another sucker punch to the belly.*

Now here she was, back in the safety of their home. Back in the sweet room they had created for her. Taking her shirt off, she tossed it over her shoulder. A rustling sounded from behind her. Quickly turning, she scanned the room with her eyes. Completely filling the tiny desk chair the Wellings had gifted her years before, sat none other than Jesse Wellings' lanky frame.

"Oh, my goodness, Jesse!" She shouted.

With a great bang, Jesse who had been very much asleep, fell to the floor. "What happened-oh Lord! Noel!" His eyes widened once he realized she was without a shirt. "I'm sorry...so sorry!"

Turning in circles Noel searched for the shirt she'd flung from her body, "What are you doing in here?" Noel squealed. "Close your eyes, close your eyes!"

"Noel," a knock sounded at her door just seconds before Pops busted in. His white hair stuck out petrified from the top of his head. He looked as crazed as if he had taken a trip through time in a DeLorean. "Are you okay?"

"Oh no!" Noel shouted, grabbing for the comforter on her bed shielding her body. Pure embarrassment flew off her body in waves of heat.

Pops turned away quickly. "Are you okay? I won't look, are you okay?"

"Yes, just go, just go," She cried mortified.

"Okay, yes, yes, I'm gone." Mr. Wellings fled the room, shutting the door, horrified that he had caught the girl in such a compromising position. And was that his son laying on the floor?

Cocooning herself in her comforter, Noel stared down at Jesse who much to her embarrassment, was curled into a ball laughing his handsome head off.

"Gosh dang you, Jesse Wellings! What in the world are you doing?" Noel kicked him with her sockless foot.

"Ouch, don't," Jesse laughed harder trying quite unsuccessfully to protect himself from her attack.

"You scared me to death, and now I've scared Pops for life. He's seen me half naked!" Noel shrieked.

"Oh, his face," Jesse chuckled, standing to his feet. "What was worse was when he locked eyes with me...I'm going to have some explaining to do in the morning."

"Stop laughing," Noel narrowed her eyes on him. His eyes crinkled, and his laughter raucous.

"Here, put your shirt on," Jesse tossed her shirt back to her.

Noel let the shirt fall to the ground, clutching at the blanket wrapped around her body. "Turn around," Noel directed raising her brows.

Shrugging his shoulders, Jesse turned his back to Noel. The last chuckle left his chest, as he said, "Seriously, I'm sorry, I wanted to talk to you after this morning. I didn't want to leave things…"

"Turn around," Noel said once her shirt was back on.

Jesse looked into her eyes, his knees grew weak and his mouth dry. "I just wanted to say I'm sorry–"

Noel held her hand up to silence him. "Don't, please don't say that, say anything but you're sorry."

Jesse stammered, "I... I mean, it's complicated. Things with mom and Sara…You and I…I mean, we haven't spoken in years. You just left me. And," he rambled on. "I know I messed up. I wanted to look cool in front of all those jerks back then. Had you come to me yourself about the formal…You have to know, part of me was terrified."

Noel snickered, "Of what?"

"Of losing you. Any romantic feelings I may've had for you, I pushed deep down way before high school started. I couldn't risk losing you, What if things didn't work out? You were more important to me than anyone." He waved his hands wildly as he spoke. He had always done that when he was nervous or upset. She sighed, somethings never change.

He was right however. She should've come to him herself, but she had been terrified of the emotions she felt for him the emotions that were still there.

"You were the most important person to me, too. You were the only person in the world that mattered." Tears leaked from her eyes. "That's why it mattered, so much, it mattered. Jesse, you were perfect–"

"But I wasn't perfect, I'm still not. I could never live up to what and who you thought I was. You put me on this pedestal, you put my entire family on this pedestal and when one of us failed you…what happened? You dropped us and ran."

"I…Jess," Noel was at a loss for words. He was right. She had no mercy, not one ounce of forgiveness–just poof, and she was gone.

"Listen, families hurt each other sometimes, but you can't just bail out on them." Jesse said, something he wanted to say to her for years.

Noel dropped on the edge of the bed, "You're right, Jess. That's exactly what I did, and I'm sorry. I regret being gone, not calling. Do you know how lonely it's been without you by my side?"

Jesse sat on the bed beside her and took one of her hands in his. "You have no idea. There's been a gaping hole in my life since you've been gone. Until, I met Sara."

Until he met Sara, those words delivered a devastating blow to her heart. She swallowed down the bile that worked its way up her throat. "I'm sure she's been good for you."

Noel hated the way her voice trembled. She'd been hoping he'd declare his love for her and that Sara had been nothing more than a distraction. Now that she was back, she hoped he'd sweep her off her feet, and Sara would just be a memory.

"Um," Jesse cleared his throat. "After mom's heart attack, I realized life's too short. I was terrified."

"I know," Noel said softly. Lightly she touched Jesse's face. She hated the pain that weighed him down. "I know."

He dropped his head in his hands and cried, his sobs filling the room and tearing at Noel's heart. "Come here. It's okay, Jess, it's going to be okay." She pulled him into her arms and let him cry.

For several minutes they sat that way, Noel rubbing Jesse's back as she consoled him. Once he calmed down he pulled back. "Man, I'm such a mess. I can't imagine a world my mother isn't in. I want to give her something special in case she doesn't have much longer." Reaching into his pocket, he pulled out a box. A tiny black satin wrapped box.

Noel gasped. What was he doing?

"A proposal," he said.

Inside the box, nestled in snowy white silk, was the most beautiful diamond engagement ring. The stone had to of been close to a carat in size. Tiny crushed diamonds had been skillfully placed along the white gold band. It was beautiful, more extravagant than she'd have picked for herself, but she loved it nonetheless.

"Do you think Sara will love it?" He asked looking to his oldest friend for reassurance.

"Sara?" Noel asked dazed. "Oh, yes, I'm sure, she'll love it." Biting back the tears, Noel beamed at Jesse. The smile was empty. "Con... congratulations."

"Will you be my best man?" He asked, opening and closing the box over and over.

"I..." Noel hesitated, her heart turning to dust in her chest. *Was he stupid?*

"It has to happen quickly. I thought Christmas Day would be perfect. Just a small gathering of our friends and family...What do you say?"

"Jess, is there no one else?" Noel didn't want to hurt him but what he was asking was ridiculous.

"No one I'd rather have by my side than you, Noel," he grabbed her hands in his. "You are one of the most important people in my life. Now that you're back I don't plan on losing you again."

"I can't. It wouldn't be fair for me to stand there on your wedding day, by your side, hating the girl who marries you. That kiss—that kiss melted away all those years I pretended to hate you, it filled my heart with a love that so much stronger than I could have ever imagined. And to know that it meant so little to you..."

"Noel, it...it meant..." Jesse tried to explain but couldn't put the words together in his mind.

Pulling her hands away, Noel stood. "You know maybe you were right back at Mel's. I need to go. We can't do this. There can be no friendship between us anymore. I'm just a girl who fell in love with her best friend when I should have been smarter. I'll find a way to be here for Jana until I go back home. No matter how much I love you...especially because I love you, I need to distance myself from you."

"Noel," Jesse stood, his eyes frantically searching her face. "I was wrong at Mel's. Don't do this. We can work it out."

"No," she shook her head sadly. "We don't need the drama. Really, let's not hurt each other all over again." Her lower lip trembled, and all he wanted to do was to kiss her until the pain he caused was gone, until there were no more tears, or disappointment.

His eyes drooped and filled with tears, he had to let her go. It was only fair. He couldn't just bail on Sara and what they shared. "I'm sorry."

Noel wanted to ask why he was sorry, but she was afraid to hear his response. Instead she stepped close to him, placed her hand on his shoulder, and softly kissed his cheek.

"See ya around," she said hoping that if they were really meant to be together, they'd find a way one day.

Nodding his head in acceptance, he said, "If you change your mind..."

"You'll be the first to know, I promise." Noel tried her best to smile at the only man she'd ever loved. He nodded his head then quietly left the room.

I love you Jesse Wellings, she thought as he disappeared from her life once again.

CHAPTER THIRTY-THREE

Mountain Road was home to the most beautiful land that occupied Harm County. Jimmy's property was among some of her favorite. Large oaks and pines covered much of the land. She was glad he suggested a hike to clear her mind.

"He. Asked. Me. To. Be. His. Best. Man!" Noel griped to Jimmy. She kicked at a tiny pile of snow covered leaves and watched the white fluff rain back to the ground.

"Yikes," Jimmy sighing. He stopped walking and wrapped Noel in his arms. "The boy is blind or stupid, I don't know which."

"Stupid," was Noel's muffled reply. She nuzzled deeper into Jimmy's embrace wanting to hide there until she forgot all about stupid Jesse Wellings. "What was I thinking? He didn't feel that way for me then and he doesn't now..."

Jimmy pulled back, confusion covering his face. "You don't know, huh?"

"What?" Noel asked wrinkling her brow.

"When you left after graduation, he went to find you. All summer before he went to art school, he traveled to every college he could get to looking for you. He never found you that summer, but a year later he did. Saw you with some guy. He said it looked like you'd moved on. He decided the best thing to do was to let you go. He loved you enough to let you live your life. A few years later he met Sara. She filled the Noel-sized hole in his heart."

"I had no idea," Noel said. She would've asked why he didn't call, but he had. As a matter of fact, he had called so much she changed her number. It was a full year later when she finally called the Wellings and gave them her new number.

His name was Ben—the guy she dated through her early college career. He was a no-good college sorority type who got too deep into drugs and alcohol and almost pulled her down with him. Thank goodness she got out while she could. It wasn't a moment too soon because a few short weeks after their split, Ben got busted selling drugs to a teen. As far as she knew, he was still in jail.

Jimmy's voice softened, "That's what happens when you run from your problems, from those who love you. You never gave Jesse a chance to explain or apologize."

"I heard it with my own ears," she started.

"You heard a teenage boy being cornered, and he panicked. It wasn't right but that's what happened. You two went through everything together, but you let one little mistake tear you apart."

"Ouch," Noel said. Jimmy was being tough.

"Listen, I don't want to be hard on you, but you left him—all of them. There was a point he had to move on, and he did. Now, he wants you to be in his life. It may not be the way you pictured it, but he wants you back. That should count for something."

"Ugh, dang it. You're right. I'll call him tonight and tell him I'll do it." Noel sighed, resigned to her fate as Jesse's best friend/best man.

"Good girl. Now, I believe you owe me a meal after the five-star service I've lavished upon you," Jimmy's mischievous grin was contagious.

"No problem, who delivers up this stinking mountain?" Noel asked.

CHAPTER THIRTY-FOUR

"Oh, Miss Noel, I'm so glad to see you here for dinner," Marta said buzzing around the kitchen.

"I need to talk to Jesse. I have to make things right between us." Noel said her stomach twisting into knots.

"I sure hope you do. That boy's been moping around the house since you all had that 'little incident'," Marta used her fingers to make quotation marks.

"I've made a mess of things again." Noel groaned.

"The two of you are still young and have your lives ahead of you." Marta said with a swish of her hand, waving away Noel's negative thoughts.

Our lives, she thought bitterly. How badly she wanted their lives to be intertwined, but what if it wasn't to be? How would things have turned out if she'd stayed in Old Harmony instead of running?

"Hopefully, you can shake Miss Sara long enough to have your say."

"She can hear what I have to say. I'm...I'm going to support Jesse and Sara. I need him to be happy, he would...he did the same for me." Noel shrugged.

Marta stepped back, put her hands on her hips, and tisked. "No girl, what you need to do is fight for your man. You love him, and I see the way he looks at you."

"I don't think he looks at me anyway in particular Marta, just as an old friend. This isn't some movie like *My Best Friend's Wedding* or something." The truth of what she said was lost on her.

Marta huffed and rolled her eyes, "Girl, did you hear what you just said?"

"Good evening, ladies," Mr. Wellings walked in. "How are my favorite girls?"

"Could be better…" Marta said, sass heavily coating each word.

At the same time, Noel spoke through clenched teeth, "Just fine Pops." She plastered a fake smile on her face.

Both women shot each other warning glances. Mr. Wellings looked back and forth between the women and decided he didn't want to get in the middle of whatever was going on. Turning on his heels to avoid the women's gazes, Mr. Wellings walked out of the room without another word.

"Marta, stop being so weird. Mr. Wellings doesn't need to know anything for the love of—" Noel whispered harshly.

"Maybe you should stop being so stubborn." Marta mumbled fussing over the pot roast she'd just pulled from the oven.

Rolling her eyes Noel quit talking. Marta was the one being stubborn and didn't know what she was talking about.

"Oh look!" Marta said loudly, rolling her neck from side to side "Here comes Mr. Jesse now, maybe you should talk to him."

"Is Sara with him?" Noel glanced over Marta's shoulder just in time to see Jesse walk by the back window. Noel turned her back quickly, "Crap, did he see me?"

"He's about to," Marta mumbled.

Seconds later Jesse walks through the kitchen door. "Marta…" He said nodding his head. His eyes shifted to Noel. "Hey."

"Hey," she said back. "Um, do you have a minute? I wanted to talk to you."

Jesse shrugged, eyeing Marta warily he said, "Sure, how about we sit in the den?"

Noel led the way. "Have a seat," she pointed. Jesse sat at the end of the long couch and Noel chose to sit next to him.

She touched the back of his hand, "Jess—I'm sorry about the other night, I should've been more—"

"No, wait." Jesse interrupted. "I shouldn't have sprung the wedding on you like that. I just...I want you back in my life and things are happening so fast." His voice broke. "You mean a lot to me, to my family. To *our* family. I think I'm confused..."

Noel's heart melted, "You all mean the world to me, too. I wish I hadn't taken off back then. I should've given you a chance to explain."

"I wish you'd stayed too." Jesse thought about what could have been, but it was too late. He had Sara now.

"You," her voice broke. "You have my heart Jesse Wellings. I need you to know I loved you since the day we met. It was you and me. There isn't anything in this world I wouldn't do for you. And if that means being there by your side as you marry the love of your life, I'll be there."

Lacing his fingers through hers, he looked down at her hands and avoided her gaze. Lightly, he ran his thumb over the back of her hers thinking of the words she said. Marrying the love of his life...was he marrying the love of his life? Or was he letting her slip away?

What could he say? That maybe he felt the same, but he wasn't sure. They didn't know each other anymore. Sara was in his life now—and she was—what was she? She was *there*...was that enough?

Looking down at her hand, he chuckled. There, just on the top of her wrist, was two evenly spaced round scars, he touched them lightly.

"What's so funny?" Noel's eyes shimmered with tears and confusion. Surely, he wasn't laughing at her?

"Sorry, it's just these marks" He rubbed his thumb over them. "I remember that day."

Snatching her hand from his grasp, Noel glared at him. "I could've died, and here you are laughing?"

Holding his sides, Jesse's chest rumbled with laughter. "You...couldn't have...it was just a little...garter snake." He wiped tears from his eyes, attempting to take in breaths between bursts of laughter.

"Dang your hide, Jesse Wellings!, That's not what you thought back then!" Her face turned red as she scolded him. Hearing the familiar tone of aggravation in her voice sent Jesse chuckling again. How many times had she fussed at him?

Playfully, Noel swatted his arm. "I was trying to save your life you ungrateful, man child!"

Unable to fight the urge, Noel too succumbed to a fit of giggles.

Truth be told, it was her fault to start with. Jesse was an artist, and when Noel wasn't around he spent most of his time indoors. One boring summer morning, Noel drug him from the comforts of his room out into the forest. The woods bordered their town and snaked up the mountains. It was Noel's second favorite place to be.

They had a wonderful afternoon climbing trees, exploring, and splashing in the creek. It was at the creek where the problems began. Jesse had been putting his shoes back on when a green-striped garter snake slithered his way.

Afraid of imminent doom, Noel jumped over to the snake and tried to catch it before it bit her beloved friend. Her aim was off, and she startled the snake. Tt struck, biting her right on her wrist.

After it struck, it slithered away leaving two petrified children in its wake. Noel was certain that it was a poisonous creature, and Jesse just knew his friend was not long for this world. The two children howled and screamed as they made their way back home. Noel cradling her hand as if it were broken.

Mere feet from the edge of the forest, and worked up into such a state, Noel grew dizzy and sat beside a tree. Convinced his friend was dying, Jesse ran straight home shouting the whole way that Noel Miracle had been in a deadly encounter with a copperhead.

By the time he made it home, he was in such a state his mother called the police and the ambulance directing them to the area Jesse said they'd ventured.

Unfortunately, when help arrived, Noel was nowhere to be found. After taking a few minutes to compose herself she decided she wasn't going to die and went home to enjoy a Popsicle with her neighbor.

Police enforcement tore the woods apart looking for Noel, afraid a wild animal had taken off with her. Her parents were notified, and the town was in turmoil. No one even bothered to check next door to see if the girl was with her elderly neighbor who had yet to hear the news of the missing girl.

Later that night, Noel showed up at home, and her parents, although slightly relieved and very intoxicated, chose not to notify officials of their daughter's safe return. Meanwhile, Jesse stayed at home not eating, hardly talking, and completely broken-hearted.

Noel, still innocent of her situation, decided to sneak through Jesse's bedroom window to give him a scare, just for good fun. When she arrived at the Wellings' home, Jesse wasn't in his room, so she decided climb inside and wait, quite impatiently, behind his bedroom door. It took all the willpower in her tiny body to allow the giggles of mischievous glee to burst from her chest. She was gonna get Jesse good.

Minutes later, the dejected boy slunk into his room and flung himself over his bed in the depths of despair. Waiting a few seconds for dramatic effect and to get her scary voice in check, Noel picked her moment. In a soft, haunting voice Noel said, "I'm gonna get you Jesse Wellings for leaving me behind."

The small boy jumped to his feet, took one look at Noel, and passed out onto the floor. Hearing the thump, Mrs. Wellings rushed into the room. "Oh, my goodness! John come quick something's wrong with Jess…"

"I think I scared 'em," Noel said. With the devil in her eyes, she tried her best to conceal a grin. Boy, she'd never let Jesse live this down.

One look at the Wellings' faces and Noel was afraid they too would pass out. But they didn't. Instead, Jana and John swooped the child up into their arms and cried tears of joy. Next, they called the police to let them know the child had been found. When the police arrived to confirm the child was in fact safe, they scolded her something awful for not letting anyone know she was okay.

"You were something back then," Jesse howled thinking of how she teased him for months after that.

"Yes, I suppose I was," she wiped tears from her cheeks.

"Man, this feels good," Jesse said a smile covering his face.

Grinning big, Noel nodded her head. "Yeah, it really does."

"I wish…" he started.

She touched his cheek lightly, "Let's not go back there. Let's just enjoy now, the time we have here, and all the good that's to come."

His face turned serious, "With the good, comes the bad." He thought of his mother.

"Yes, but we'll make it through no matter what happens. Jana is a strong woman, and I believe she will make it through this. No matter what, you won't have to go through it alone. I won't leave you again. I'm hear as much as you need me."

"He won't be needing you. He has me." The nasally voice that snarled from behind made the pair both pull back from one another.

Sara, in her exquisite beauty, glared at them her arms crossed over her chest. She would've been much more beautiful if the hate-filled sneer that crossed her face wasn't a permanent fixture to her features.

"You're right, I just meant–" Noel started.

"I know what you meant, and I see what you're doing. How could you take advantage of him like this? He's at his weakest, most vulnerable point in life and here you are throwing yourself at him like some...trailer trash–I would say prostitute but that would be to classy for a girl like you." Sara looked at Noel as if she were dog mess on her shoe. She thought she was better than Noel.

Maybe she was, Noel thought.

Noel stood, holding her head high., Through clenched teeth she said, "I'm sorry you feel that way, Sara. You're right., I only meant I'd be here for you both when the time arises. Please forgive me for how this must've looked," Noel pointed to her and Jesse. "Now, if you'd excuse me."

Her nails cut into her fist, and she bit her bottom lip so hard she tasted blood. The trailer park side of her wanted to hurdle the couch and slap some manners into the girl, but for Jesse's sake, she'd refrain...she'd do anything for him.

"Noel..." Jesse started, popping to his feet. Sara's head snapped his way. He looked at the fierce young woman then back to Noel. "Thank you."

Noel nodded, turned on her heel, and walked away. Sara had a right to be upset. After all, Noel was in love with her man. *Oh, the web we weave,* she thought bitterly.

*   *   *

Intense shouting was heard through the Wellings' home that night. Noel wisely stayed in her room until she heard the front door slam, and the home once again grew quiet. She waited a few breaths then popped her head into the hallway.

She saw Jesse open his mother's bedroom door then slide in. She caught just a tiny glimpse of his face, and it broke her heart.

I'm making everything worse, she thought. With a heavy heart she knew what she needed to do, what he had once done for her. She'd always be there for him, but he needed space. Her presence was bringing back too many memories, and Sara was right. Her being there was messing with Jesse when he was at his most vulnerable. She had to let him go.

It didn't take long to pack her bags, or to write a note of goodbye. She promised to visit on Christmas as it was just a few days away. She couldn't disappoint Jana. That was all she could give them now. She wouldn't be the reason Jesse and Sara fell apart. It was better this way, for all of them.

CHAPTER THIRTY-FIVE

Sitting in her regular booth at Mel's, Noel shoved handfuls of greasy fries into her mouth. She tried to ignore the soulful tones of *Blue Christmas*. She barely chewed as the grease-coated potatoes brought a small amount of comfort to her miserable life.

"Where will you go?" Jimmy asked over a piping hot cup of black coffee. His eyes widening as he watched Noel eat her feelings.

Noel sighed deeply. "I haven't figured that out yet. If I go all the way back home, I won't make it back to see Jana for Christmas. There's a little motel I saw on the other side of the— what—why are you making that face?"

"You're not staying in that motel," Jimmy looked around the crowded café lowering his voice, "They make meth there."

Noel whooped, she could always count on Jimmy for a laugh. "What kind of nonsense–"

"Just stay with me." He shrugged.

"I couldn't...it wouldn't be proper...besides I can't take advantage of your kindness. You've done enough for me already."

Jimmy shook his head, "Really, I won't be home much. The holiday hours are insane, even for a small-town pharmacy such as mine. And besides Gunner could use a pal to keep him company. You'd be doing me a favor if you'd keep an eye on the little guy for me."

Noel groaned, "Why'd you have to bring Gunner into this…You know I love that crazy bundle of chocolate fur."

"Yeah, I think he loves you more than me, the traitor," Jimmy said in mock sadness.

Noel rolled her eyes, "Whatever! You two are like each other's spirit animals."

He chuckled, "True, so what do you say? You can have the guest room. I promise I won't even hit on you."

"Really…" Noel raised her brows.

"Nope not even a little. I like the small evil brunette types. Ugh, platinum blond is so 1990's!" He said with an over-exaggerated eye roll.

Noel laughed and tossed a fry at his head. "You're impossible!"

With quick reflexes Jimmy opened his mouth and caught the fry. "Yeah, I kind of am!" He agreed loudly chomping the hot fry.

"Well, for Gunner's sake, I'll accept your offer and keep him company until after Christmas." Noel agreed taking a large gulp of her strawberry and chocolate milk shake.

Noel's phone chirped. Looking down she sighed, "It's Jana…I'll call her later." She silenced the phone.

"You have to talk to them sooner or later." Jimmy wiggled his eyebrows.

"Not now. I don't know what to say…*hey, I love your son, so I can't come around and be a witness to his happy occasion.*" Noel sulked then raised her empty cup letting Mel know she was ready for a refill.

"Okay, I'm not going to push you on it, but Jana asked for you to be here. She's missed you, and it's not fair to pull another disappearing act on her of all people. She shouldn't have to suffer because you and Jesse can't get it together." This time he gave her a serious pointed look.

"Ya boy here isn't wrong," Mel said sliding a fresh milkshake across the table and collecting the dirty glass. "Not to mention you and that boy have had the hots for each other since grade school and that hasn't changed no matter what either of you say."

Jimmy cocked his head to the side and stared at Noel with a pointed look—*you going to argue with Mel like you do with me?*

"Oh, shut it Jim-Bo! And thanks Mel, you've always given it to me straight. I just don't want to be the cause of Jesse and Sara's problems, you know?"

"So, you'd rather him marry a retched hag like that and both you be miserable the rest of your days?"

Jimmy laughed at Mel's bluntness, "Oh Mel, where've you been all my life? Marry me!"

"Watch it son, I'll make an honest man out of ya real quick," Mel shot him a denture-filled smile and cackled her way back to the kitchen.

"From the mouth of Mel!" Noel shook her head. "Jim, I really can't say anything else or do anything about Jesse. He knows how I feel now, and he still wants to marry Sara."

"Yeah, you're probably right." He said evenly taking a giant sip of his coffee. Noel could tell he didn't agree but he didn't push the issue either.

"So anyway, you sure you don't mind me staying?" She asked.

"No, I wouldn't mind you staying around these parts forever. It's been so good having you around even if you won't love me." Jimmy teased.

"You're ridiculous. I've enjoyed spending time with you too. Honestly, I stay to myself so much at home that the thought of returning fills me with dread. I forgot how lucky I was here." Noel admitted.

"I know you weren't interested in a teaching position here, but Mrs. Craig is about to retire from Mercer Elementary. I mean, it's about twenty mins out from here but not too bad." Jimmy offered.

"Isn't she the principal?" Noel asked confused.

"Yeah,, but you could do it easy. I bet you'd be great at the job. You went off and got that fancy Master's degree and all—it would be a shame not to put it to good use." He answered.

"I don't know…it'd be hard leaving my kids and being this close to Jesse and Sara." she grumbled.

"Yeah but also close to me, Jana, and Mr. W. I mean if Jana has her surgery then she'll need you to keep her company." Jimmy pressed.

"I don't know, I'll think about it. It just seems unlikely that they'd pick me. I haven't been teaching that long and they may want someone with more experience."

Jimmy shrugged. "You're young, energetic, and full of great ideas. They'd be foolish to not hire you. Plus, I have a few friends on the board. I could put in a good word."

"Do it you crazy girl!" Mel screeched from the behind the counter as she pretended to wipe it down with a washcloth.

Noel laughed, "You know what, I may check it out, just to see what they say. What can it hurt?"

"Let me make a call for you. Everyone's on break for the holiday, but I heard they wanted a replacement ASAP to train with Mrs. Craig for the rest of the year. I'm sure they'd give you time to get your affairs in order before you start."

"Why not? What could it hurt?" Noel laughed wondering how Jimmy talked her into this.

CHAPTER THIRTY-SIX

Jesse sat in the waiting area with his father as Jana had her consult for surgery. The wait was excruciating as he and his father sat in perfect silence waiting for what felt like an eternity. The men had been sitting for over thirty minutes before his father broke the silence.

"Son, I don't like to stick my nose where it doesn't belong, but I feel I wouldn't be doing my duty as your father if I didn't at least share my feelings with you on something." Mr. Wellings said turning to his son.

Jesse looked at his father confused. "What is it Pops?"

"Well, it's Noel...she's been on my mind the last few days. She didn't say why she left, but I have a pretty good hunch it has a little something to do with you and maybe a lot to do with Sara. Am I right?"

Jesse's body sagged, "I'm pretty sure it has everything to do with me and Sara."

"You want to talk about it?" Mr. Wellings asked.

"I...I think I've made a terrible mistake. I told her I was going to ask Sara to marry me, but I can't Pops. Just spending time with Noel has me reconsidering being with Sara at all. I don't have feelings for Sara like I do for Noel."

"I see," his father said. "Does Sara or Noel know how you feel?"

Jesse took in a deep breath, "No, I don't want to hurt Noel more than I already have. I took the ring I bought for Sara back to Murphy's Jewelry. I think I'm going to end things with her, but I wanted to wait until after Christmas. It seems like a poor time to break up if I do it before."

"What happened with you and Noel all those years ago? Did you have a fight or something?" His father asked.

Ashamed of himself but needing to confess, he finally let the story out. He told his father how he loved Noel from early on and how he hid those feelings deep down to keep from ruining their friendship. He confessed to his part in hurting Noel many years ago. "And to make it worse, I kissed her the other day, and I think it messed us both up."

Mr. Wellings patted his sons' knee, "Well son, when it comes to the women we love, I suppose we men are a bit of a mess. I was like that with you mother. I was a dumb young man in college, and she was a beautiful queen. It took me a while to get things right with her. I almost lost her completely to some jerk on the football team. I had to beg her to go on a date with me, and I never left her side since then. I guess we have the dumb gene son."

Jesse chuckled, "I didn't know that about you and mom. What would you do it you were me?"

"What does your heart say?" His father asked.

"Noel, always Noel, but what if I upset her and she leaves again? I don't think I could stand it." Tears filled Jesse's eyes as he remembered the betrayal and rejection he felt when Noel cut him completely off all those years ago.

"Either way son, if you don't truly love Sara, you should let her know." His father said.

Jesse ran his hands through his hair. "I know. Man, it's going to make work complicated that's for sure."

"Yeah son...it just might. Maybe she'll move on if you're not together." His father offered.

"Maybe– "Jesse started but was interrupted by Dr. Sanderson's nurse.

"Gentlemen, can you all come back for a moment? Jana wants you with her," she said.

The men shared a worried look with one another. Simultaneously, they stood and followed the nurse into the room where the woman whom they both dearly loved waited for them.

Jana smiled warmly at the men who made up her world. Where had time gone she thought, looking at the handsome young man Jesse had grown to become. She prayed that if things went wrong with her health that her son would have as happy of a life with his future spouse as she had had with his father.

"Boys, we need to talk," she said, tears filling her eyes.

CHAPTER THIRTY-SEVEN

Noel darted into the pharmacy, a Cheshire grin spread across her face. Glancing around the store she looked for Jimmy, but he was nowhere to be found.

"Can I help you miss?" Julie, the pharmacy tech on duty, asked Noel.

"Oh, yes, I was looking for Jim. Is he around?" She asked.

The girl shook her head. "He ran down to Mel's to grab dinner for us. Can I leave him a message, or would you like to wait? I'm sure he won't be long."

"Um, yeah, I'll wait. I have something to tell him." Noel answered the smile still in place. Her jaws almost hurt from her joy, but she couldn't turn it down.

Her purse buzzed. Digging around, she looked for her phone. The one person that could wipe the smile from her face was the one person whose phone number popped up on her screen. Didn't Jesse get it? She needed time to clear her head.

She told Pops she'd spend Christmas Eve with him and Momma Jay. She'd spend Christmas Day alone with Gunner wishing bad thoughts upon Jesse's new bride. She wanted to be happy for Jesse, and she expected that one day she'd be. However, in that moment, she couldn't bear to even hear his voice.

Powering her phone off, she slid it back in her purse.

"Hey lady! Are you here with some good news, or did you just miss me?" Jimmy's voice boomed from behind.

"Very good!" Noel could barely conceal her glee turning to him.

Jimmy breezed by her heading for the break room. "Come on back. We can share some fries while you tell me all about it."

On his heels, Noel followed him to the back of the store. The break room had changed from when she was a child. It was the one place Jimmy had updated. He painted the walls muted gray, posters of sports teams adorned the walls, and right behind the break table, mounted to the wall, a fifty-inch flat panel television played an endless stream of sporting events.

"Nice," Noel said, knowing she and Jesse would've enjoyed a room like that when they were kids. Instead, when they went to the pharmacy, they were put to work or had to finish homework in the breakroom. Back then, the room held only an old wood table and two hard chairs.

"I spend so much time here I had to have a place to chill every now and then," Jimmy confessed. "Anyways, how was the interview?"

"It was great. I mean, I went in not expecting much but Jimmy, the pay is double what I make now. And you were right! They're looking for someone younger to come in with fresh ideas."

"And…" Jimmy prodded shoving a fistful of fries in his mouth.

"And they said they were afraid I was much too young for the position. They said they would call me and let me know." She said then hesitated.

Jimmy looked at her out of the corner of his eye. "Why are you holding info from me?"

Noel laughed, "You know me too well. Well, I hadn't gotten out of the parking lot when I got a call from Mark Janson, the head of the board, and he offered me the assistant principal position. He said Terry Sprouse was going to take the head principal position, but I would be a perfect fit to be her assistant!"

Her squeal of joy brought a smile to his face. "Good girl! When do you start?"

"Well, I have to call my boss and see what he needs me to do. They've been good to me there, and I can't just leave them hanging. So, it's up in the air, but I should be able to start early February if all goes well." Noel sighed thinking of all the work she had to do.

"I'm glad you stopped by to let me know. Are you going to the hospital

129

now? If you wait about an hour, I can go with you. Jana would love some good news right about now."

"The hospital?" Noels face paled.

Jimmy raised his eyebrows, "Yeah Jana should be out of surgery by now."

"Surgery?" Noel asked sinking in her chair.

"Yeah, didn't anyone call you?" Jimmy wiped his chin with a napkin. "When I saw Jesse this morning, he said they'd call you. I mean everything happened quickly, but I figured by now—"

Noel took in a deep breath closing her eyes. "Jesse had been calling all day, but I didn't answer. I needed…"

"It's okay. I'm sure Jana's fine. Tell you what, Julie's more than capable of taking care of everything. I'll see if she minds closing up, and then we can head over to the hospital together. While I get everything in order, call Jesse and find out where everyone is and how Jana is doing. We can head out in a few mins."

Noel's lower lip trembled. What if it were too late? What if something had happened and that's why Jesse had been calling?

"Don't get worked up yet, okay?" Jimmy gave her a quick hug. "I'll be right back."

Nodding Noel's fingers trembled as she held the power button down on her phone. The wait for the phone to power back on felt like an eternity.

Her phone buzzed several times indicating she had several voicemails. All from Jesse. She decided to call him directly instead of listening to his messages. He answered after the first ring.

"Noel?" he said his voice coated with exhaustion.

"Yes, it's me, sorry I missed you. How is Momma Jay?" She asked her body trembling.

"She's…she's okay. Surgery went well, and she's in a medically-induced coma so she can rest."

"Oh good, thank God!" Noel breathed a breath of relief. "I'm on my way up there in just a few minutes."

"Okay, we are in room 549 in the cardiac unit." He answered instantly, relieved to hear her voice.

"See you soon, goodbye," Noel said softly.

*   *   *

130

"You doing okay?" Mr. Wellings asked his son

It was hard on Jesse to see his mother in such a state. The strong-willed woman they loved lay before them sick and frail. A tube down her throat attached to a machine by her bed breathed for her as she slumbered in a drug stupor. They said she was doing well, and if she continued to breathe well on the machine, by morning she could have the tube removed. Having the tube removed was just the beginning of a long road to recovery.

"I'm good Pops," Jesse turned his tired eyes to his father.

Black bags encircled the eyes of both men. The two men who depended on Jana's constant love and support were uncertain of what the future held. How could she go through so much and bounce back to the woman she once was? Was it even possible?

"Is Sara going to make it up tonight?" His father asked.

Jesse pushed air through his teeth, "I went to see her last night to tell her about mom and–I don't know. For the first time I think I saw what everyone else saw. She was cold and indifferent. She just wasn't–to be honest she wasn't Noel. So, I took your advice and followed my heart. I was honest with her. She deserves better than what I could give her. Oddly, she seemed relieved to be rid of me. It hurts a little too let go of a big piece of my life, but I think we are both far from devastated."

Mr. Wellings placed a hand on his sons' shoulder. "I'm sorry to hear, it but it sounds like you did the right thing. Momma will be proud of you."

"Pssh, Momma will be ready to plan a wedding for me and Noel if she can. To her credit, she tries not to say anything, but she drops some pretty serious hints to our future."

Mr. Wellings chuckled, "Yes, your mother can be pretty bold when she wants."

Shaking his head Jesse gave a little laugh as well, "Yeah she can, but that dream may not come true to either of us. Noel will barely talk to me. I doubt she would've called me at all if Momma hadn't had surgery."

"Give her time son, she may come around. Not to mention she must still believe you and Sara are an item, a soon-to-be-married item if I'm not mistaken." Looking up Mr. Wellings spied Noel coming down the hallway her arm looped through Jimmy Wren's. "Speaking of the angel," Mr. Wellings walked to the door and waved Noel in.

"There's my girl!" He wrapped her in a hug. "Jimmy," he stepped back and shook Jim's hand.

Jesse had to bite back his words seeing the pair together. Jimmy and Noel sure didn't waste time. He heard Noel was staying at Jimmy's place. The hard fist of jealousy sucker punched him straight in the gut.

"I need some air," Jesse dashed from the room.

"Is he okay?" Noel asked her brow creased in concern.

She followed Jesse with her eyes until he was out of sight. His gait was rigid, and shoulders pulled in together tightly.

"Oh, I reckon he will be. He just had a rough day is all." Mr. Wellings answered. "Come on in. She won't wake until morning, but I'm sure she'll be glad to know you two were here."

"So, what happened? I didn't think she could have surgery until after the first of the year." Noel asked.

"Yes, she was scheduled for January 5th but there was a cancellation and with her condition the doctor decided to move her up."

Noel looked concerned, "Will she be okay?"

Mr. Wellings shrugged, "They say surgery went well, and that she's doing as well as can be expected. To be honest, the doctors were clear about the risk of surgery with her, but she did wonderfully. If she continues with no issues tonight, they'll remove the tube, so she can breathe on her own. And if she does well, the doctor said she can go home on Christmas Eve."

"What!?! Isn't that soon?" Noel crossed her arms over her chest, wondering what the doctors were thinking.

"No, not by today's standards." Mr. Wellings explained. "Now they say it's better to recover at home. Staying in the hospital too long can cause more trouble than good. Higher risk of infections or something."

"I guess if she feels up to it, being home for Christmas would be nice," Noel said uncertainly.

Looking at Jana hooked to machines, tubes, and wires, she wondered how in the world Momma Jay would be ready to come home so soon. "It's her favorite," she said. Thinking of Christmas' past Noel began to cry. Loud sobs racked her body as she walked to the woman and grabbed her hand.

Jimmy followed rubbing her back while she cried. Everyone stayed that way for a long time, the room silent except the insistent beeping of the overhead monitors. Memories of years past flooded Noel, and she was grateful for the new job opportunity that came her way.

No matter how she felt in the past, this was home and these people her family. She'd find a way to prepare her heart to see Jesse and Sara together when they ran into each other in town. Who knows, once she got settled maybe she'd find her life partner and those feelings she had for Jesse would fade.

"Pops, can I do anything for you?" Noel asked suddenly realizing how hard this had to be for him.

"No dear, I'm fine. It's getting late though. Maybe you should go home and get some rest." Mr. Wellings dropped, exhausted into a reclining chair.

"How about you go home, and I stay here?" Noel offered.

Mr. Wellings held his arms up and shook his head. "Oh no, I'd never be able to sleep without her by my side."

Noel smiled, "God love you, Pops. I'll come back in the morning, how about that?"

"That'll be perfect, Jana will want to see you as soon as possible young lady." Mr. Wellings said in mock sternness.

"Yes sir!" Noel said. "I can't wait to share my good news with her!"

"Good news? We can all use a little of that around here." He answered.

"Keep it a secret but I'll be moving to Mercer at the beginning of the year. I got the assistant principal position at Mercer Elementary." Noel bounced on her toes with excitement.

Jimmy chimed in, wrapping his arm around her shoulder and giving her a big squeeze. "Can't let this one go! I need her in my life."

Mr. Wellings eyes filled with tears of joy, "Well that's certainly wonderful news! Jana will be over the moon to hear this. Thank you, Jimmy, for doing what we couldn't and getting our girl home."

Jimmy beamed, "I don't know how I'd live without her now."

A sniffle from the door had the group swivel to see who had arrived. Jesse was back, his hands clenched in fists watching the pair share Noel's "good news."

"Congratulations," Jesse said through clenched teeth. *First, she moves in with the guy and then she moves her entire life back home for him?* Jesse fumed. At one point he had been her best friend and she dropped him without a care in the world.

Noel wrinkled her brow, "Thanks?" She said confused by the mixed signal he was sending out.

Jesse turned to his dad, "Pops, I'm gonna scoot. I have some stuff I need to take care of at home."

"Okay son, I'll see you in the morning." Mr. Wellings said confusion covering his face as well.

Once out of ear shot, Jimmy asked, "You sure he's okay?"

"Oh yes, yes. he's tired is all." Mr. Wellings said watching his son's retreating back, he was unable to conceal the doubt that covered his face.

"You sure I can't stay so you can get some rest yourself?" Noel asked opening her arms to hug Pops once again.

"Absolutely!" The older man said hugging her tight. "Now scoot, you two!"

Noel broke from his embrace and turned to leave. Before Jesse's weird behavior her heart had been a little lighter but now she was confused and hurt that he didn't share her joy in returning home. Maybe her being close made him uneasy.

Shrugging off his odd behavior, Noel chose to bask in her good news and push Jesse Wellings far from her mind.

CHAPTER THIRTY-EIGHT

Jesse slammed the door to his office shut. He was too wound up to go home. He needed to work. It was paint or go back to the hospital and take on Jimmy Wren. Seeing as how Jimmy's bicep was as big around as Jesse's head, he decided he'd beat up a canvas instead.

Thank goodness he kept extra clothing in the office for days when he wanted to blow off steam. Dating a girl like Sara meant many late nights in the studio. And that was another thing…he ended his relationship with Sara because he couldn't keep Noel off his mind and what does she do? Runs off with Jimmy-stinking-Wren…Old Harmony's bachelor of the year! And how could she move her whole life back to Mercer of all places?

Slapping the canvas with as much gusto as he could, Jesse painted fervently. He was a mad man with a paint brush. Aggressively, he mixed colors and slapped his brush against the saturated canvas.

What was so great about Jimmy anyways? Sure, he was good looking, rich, funny, and if he were being honest with himself, Jimmy was a heck of a good guy. He sure had been good to Jesse's parents and had taken amazing care of the pharmacy. All the customers loved the guy.

Jesse liked him until the first time he saw Noel dangling from his muscular arm. Lava like rage boiled in his chest as he thought of the pair together.

Looking at his watch, he was surprised to see it was after four in the morning. It was pointless to go back home to rest. Rubbing the sleep from his face, he admired his work. Shaking his head, he wondered if he'd ever have peace.

The canvas was, of course, Noel. Her soulful, gray eyes stared back at him, causing an ache deep in his gut, and a desire to make her his stirred in his chest. How had things gone so wrong? She'd been his everything. Too bad he had been too stupid to realize her value before it was too late.

Without cleaning his supplies, something he never did, he turned off the lights and locked up his shop. He needed to do the one thing that was more important than fixating on Noel and that was to visit his mother and wait for the doctors to evaluate her progress.

CHAPTER THIRTY-NINE

Noel shivered and pressed her hand to the air vent, her skin screaming for warmth. The air outside had dropped a good twenty degrees since the sun had gone down.

"Did you get a weird vibe from Jesse tonight? I mean...I know he's worried about Momma Jay, but he seemed..."

Jimmy cut her off, "like he wanted to punch my lights out?"

"Well, um yeah, that's exactly what I thought. Are you and Jesse on bad terms or anything?" Noel asked.

"I wasn't until I moved in on his girl." Jimmy joked.

Her eyes grew wide pretending astonishment, "Sara Rhymes? Why Jimmy, you are a deviant."

Jimmy laughed, "No you twit, you...I believe be doesn't like seeing you," he tweaked her nose before putting both hands back on the steering wheel, "with me!"

"Whatever! I can't deal with Jesse right now. There's too much other stuff going on. Besides if he's going to marry that sweet angel of a girl Sara Rhymes, then he needs to get me out of his head."

Wisely, Jimmy didn't say anything, but he wondered if Jesse Wellings would in fact wed Sara or if he'd use his brain and snatch up Noel before it was too late.

He shook his head wishing he had a chance with her himself, but he rather enjoyed their friendship. If truth be told, he still needed time to heal from losing Jennifer. Noel's friendship had certainly helped with the process. He was immensely grateful that the stars aligned, and Noel was moving back home.

"What has you looking so serious?" Noel's eyes twinkled from the moon beams that cut through the night.

"Just that I'm grateful for having you back in my life." Jimmy said giving her a chummy shove in the shoulder.

"I don't see how you could stand me when I out-do you in everything," Noel jeered.

Jimmy pouted. "Not true!"

"Oh yeah, name one thing your better at–" Noel prodded.

Quickly he cut in, "Cooking!"

Noel's jaw dropped in shocked outrage, "Talk about hitting where it hurts-*ouch*-you've been waiting to use that one haven't you?"

"Well, your highness, you needed to be reminded that there are some things in this world you stink at!" Jimmy taunted.

"I never! How we've stayed friends so long is beyond me!" Noel cackled.

"Cause no one else will have ya," he shot back.

"Humph," Noel grunted.

"As much as I enjoy us tearing each other's self-esteem down...we have other important matters to discuss." Jimmy grew serious again.

"Such as?" she asked.

"Such as a certain girls' birthday is coming up and we need to celebrate." Jimmy reminded her.

"Oh yeah," she'd almost forgotten.

How could she celebrate her birthday knowing Jesse was marrying Sara that very day? Did Jesse even think of that when he planned the wedding date?

Reading the instantaneous sagging of her body, Jimmy got it. Once again, he thought Jesse Wellings was an idiot.

"Tell you what? How about a quiet evening at home and a movie? I plan to have the pharmacy open half a day, but I mean there's not much else going to be happening in town on Christmas Day anyways." Jimmy offered.

"That sounds perfect," Noel grinned at him gratefully.

"Then it's a date! I will close the pharmacy around six if it is dead and then I'm all yours!"

Noel smiled, but the intense clenching inside her gut was almost unbearable. She couldn't wait to get inside the guest room at Jimmy's house and allow herself a good cry for what she'd missed. She hated the beautiful brunette for living the life Noel had always dreamed of.

CHAPTER FORTY

Jesse arrived back at the hospital before five am after a night of painting and no sleep. It had felt good to let his aggression out on the canvas, but frustration still clung to his skin.

Frustrated he couldn't love Sara, and frustrated because he did love Noel. He was even more furious when he thought of Noel in the arms of Jimmy the giant pharmacist.

"You may want to loosen your grip on that Styrofoam cup, son, or you're going to regret it shortly." Mr. Wellings warned, watching his son take his frustrations out on the drinkware.

Too late, Jesse's fingers pressed through the cup and the nuclear hot liquid flowed down his hands and wrists.

"Oh, son of a... dang it!" He shouted barely concealing the curse he badly wanted to let out.

His mother shifted in her bed and moaned. Instant guilt flooded his heart. "Sorry Momma," he wasn't sure if she could understand him through the drugs that ran through her veins. However, if she could hear him she'd give him a talking to.

Without saying a word, his father grabbed a handful of paper towels from the bathroom dispenser and crouched over to mop up the mess. Jesse stayed in his seat, his head bowed. For reasons unbeknownst to him, he began to cry.

Forgetting about the mess, his father dropped the paper towels and pulled his son into a tight embrace. "Oh, buddy, it's okay, it's okay. There now, what's this about?"

"God, I'm sorry," Jesse sniffled and wiped his eyes with the back of his hand. "I'm such a mess. I guess I'm tired and have a lot on my plate right now." Jesse sighed, embarrassed by his display of emotions.

"It's okay, I can't tell you how many breakdowns I've had since your Momma's been sick, but I don't think this breakdown is entirely about your mother is it?" His father asked pointedly.

"No, I don't think it is Pops. It's Noel. I've tried everything I could to get her out of my mind. I almost proposed to Sara hoping that if I totally moved on I could get her out of my head. I even told Noel that Sara and I'd be married on Christmas Day." Jesse shared.

"And she doesn't know that you two have split up? Hmmm, no wonder she left our house. She was protecting you," Mr. Wellings shared with great insight.

Jesse tilted his head confused, "Protecting me?"

John Wellings smiled at his naive son. "She didn't want to cause trouble for you and your bride. Not to mention she accepted the assistant principal's position."

"Yeah, I heard her say she accepted a job in Mercer." Jesse's head buzzed from lack of sleep.

Just the thought of seeing Noel and Jimmy together all over town made him sick to his stomach. *Maybe I should take off to New York and just immerse myself into the art scene for a bit*, he thought.

"Don't tell your mother. Noel wants to surprise her." his father said with a smile.

His parents loved Noel, he loved Noel, and apparently Jimmy did as well. *How did that ape win her heart?* Jesse wondered bitterly.

"I won't...when is moms' doctor due in for her checkup?" He asked.

"Um, they said before breakfast, but who really knows with these places. Why don't you go take a shower and grab a cup of real coffee, preferably in a cup you can't smash with your bare hands? By the time you get back, the doctor will have visited, and we can see what we need to do from there."

"Are you sure?" Jesse asked.

"Son, I insist. You look a mess...and you slightly smell." His father said helping his son to his feet.

Jesse wrinkled his nose as he smelled himself. "Yup, I do. Okay I'll go, but I'll be back in a few hours. I'll go by Mel's for coffee. She makes that stuff strong enough to stand your hair on end."

"I think I may need that today. Love you son, be careful," his dad patted his shoulder as they hugged goodbye.

John Wellings watched his son leave the ICU, a broken-hearted young man. He trusted that things would work themselves out for Jesse and Noel. Whatever happened, he loved them both dearly and hoped this whole mess wouldn't end in disaster.

Looking over at the woman who'd given him much joy over the last forty years he wished both those kids would find what he and Jana had shared. Only God knew what the future held for those two. Now all he could do was pray.

CHAPTER FORTY-ONE

Noel woke before the sun rose to take a shower. She was excited to see that more snow had fallen. Every surface of the land was draped in pearly white flakes. She'd forgotten how beautiful Old Harmony was in the winter. From her room, she could see the town below, and it was a sight to behold. She had always wondered what the view was like from where she stood, and it was amazing. God's handywork was simply beautiful!

The moon had begun to fade away, giving the sun room to light the sky. It was still dim enough, however, that Noel could see the Christmas lights that adorned the entire downtown square. One night soon she'd need to take a night ride around town and enjoy the sweet little town before the decorations came down.

Sighing, she realized she'd need to get a better vehicle if she was to drive around Old Harmony at all in the winter, especially while she stayed on Mountain Road with Jimmy. Enough snow and ice had fallen to keep her from driving her little sports car down the mountain. She'd have to hitch a ride with Jimmy to the hospital. She so badly wanted to see Jana fully awake.

The scuffling of fuzzy feet and long puppy nails scuffled across the hardwood floors. Jimmy and Gunner must be up for the day. Jim usually got to the pharmacy early in the morning and worked late into the evening.

He really was a wonderful, hardworking man, and not for the first time she wanted to kick her own behind for not being able to love him as she should.

Maybe one day...one day when she'd gotten tired of seeing Sara Rhymes on Jesse's arms. Or maybe when they had perfect little Jesse and Sara-mixed babies. Or perhaps she'd die an old crazy cat lady. She chuckled at the thought. She really wasn't a cat person. Maybe she'd get her a pup like Gunner to keep her company when she moved.

A pang of anxiety ran through her body as she thought of moving to Mercer and being alone again. She hadn't realized how lonely she'd been until coming back home. Being around Jimmy, Jana, and John had reminded her of how much she needed people in her life.

"Coffee?" Jimmy asked peeking his head into her room.

"I could've been changing!" Noel said turning from the window.

"Pity you weren't," Jimmy fired back the devil in his eyes.

Shaking her head Noel chastised him, "The woman who does land you will have her hands full, buddy."

"That she will...so is that a no on the coffee?" Jimmy picked.

"Uh, that will be a yes for the coffee, and can I get a ride into town to see Jana on your way to work? I can get a cab back later. I just don't want to take the 'stang down these hills and curves."

"How about you drop me off at work and borrow the truck for the day? I get off early today. You can pick me up around four if that works for you?" He asked.

"That'll be perfect! I need to go check out an apartment in Mercer. It's just down the road from the school, and its reasonably priced." She said mentally planning her day.

"Sure, but don't feel like you have to make a rash decision on where to stay. Mi casa, su casa senorita."

Noel laughed, "Pulling out all that fancy language...not bad, sir, not bad."

Jimmy walked away but said over his shoulder, "Get ready you ingrate, breakfast is in five."

* * *

Riding the elevator to the ICU, Noel's palms sweated and her stomach churned. She hated hospitals. She knew they were good and helped people who needed medical attention, but they made her sad. She thought of how much pain, anguish, and despair the walls of the building had experienced. She also thought of losing Jana. Vivid images of finding a crushed Jesse and John Wellings after being told Jana hadn't made it through the night filled her mind.

She knew they would've called her and told her if something had happened, but still those images filled her mind. The elevator lurched and then stopped. The overhead bell rang, and the doors glided open. Noel exited the tiny cart that opened to a large waiting room.

"Oh crap," Noel mumbled turning her face from the couple who stood just outside the elevator cart.

Sara and Jesse stood alone wrapped in each other's arms. Sara's back was to the elevator, but Jesse faced it. His eyes lingered on Noel for a second before quietly whispering words of encouragement to Sara.

She must've been upset about Jana. Noel's heart dropped. Had something happened? Without a second glance at the couple, Noel charged to Jana's room. What would she find?

Flying into the room at full steam and her eyes wide, Noel took in the scene before her.

Jana sat propped up in bed, the tube from her throat gone, eating what looked like orange sherbet ice cream. The television blared one of Jana's favorite games shows she'd watched since Noel was a child.

"Mamma Jay? Are you–" Noel took a few cautious steps into the room.

Holding her arms out for a hug, Jana said in a slightly-hoarse voice, "Right as rain, my love!"

Gently Noel hugged Jana. "I was so worried. I saw Jesse and Sara and she looked so upset...I was afraid..."

Jana stiffened, "Sara? Oh, she must just be a bit overwhelmed. I'm fine, see?"

Jana shot her husband a look over Noel's head that said, *let's stay out of this.* John nodded his head agreeably. He wanted nothing more than to let the kids work things out on their own.

"Yeah, I suppose she has a lot on her plate." Noel said fairly. Planning a last-minute Christmas wedding had to be stressful.

Pulling back, Noel sat in a rocker chair beside Jana's bed staying close enough to hold the dear woman's hand in her own. "John tells me you have some good news for me, but he said I'd have to wait for you to share it. I've been waiting in pure torture for you to arrive."

Noel's eyes crinkled in delight at being able to share her news with Jana. "Well, you're looking at the new assistant principal for Mercer Elementary!"

Jana tilted her head, thinking through the girl's words. It took a few seconds before complete understanding registered in her mind. "Oh, oh, oh John! Our Noel's coming home, for good!"

Her husband's eyes watered as he watched his wife's face light up. Noel was a beacon of hope and love for his family, and they were relieved she'd be back close to home.

Holding Noel at arm's length to look at the girl, Jana said, "I'm so happy you'll be so close to us. You can stay with us while you look for a permanent home you know."

Noel's cheeks turned red, "I know. It's just that Jimmy has offered me his guest room and he's a bit closer to Mercer..." And he doesn't have Jesse Wellings parading in and out of his house with his soon-to-be wife.

Jana's face fell temporarily in disappointment, but she quickly recovered. She knew the real reason Noel chose not to stay with them any longer. With any luck that would all change soon, unless her son was too thick to make the right decision.

"Of course, dear, I hear he has plenty of room as well. When do you start at Mercer?" Jana asked.

"I have to go back for a few weeks after the New Year until my old job finds a replacement, and I have to pack my things. I plan to be back by the beginning of February."

"I'm so glad to hear that. You better not become a stranger living so close," the woman admonished.

"Never," Noel squeezed Jana's hand gently. "I'm sorry for how negligent I've been the last several years. I'll never do that again. It's been lonely without you all."

"I'm glad to hear it! Now moving on to some more important business–Christmas dinner!"

"Oh, but Jesse's wedding...I didn't think..."

Jana raised her voice over the girl's, "Wedding or not, we'll have Christmas dinner and of course your birthday favorite–baked Alaska. It's time to get back to tradition. Marta has agreed to prepare the meal for us a head of time, but I'll need your help warming it all back up."

"I don't mind helping, but are you sure you'll feel up to having something like that after the wedding? That's a big day for anyone but after surgery..."

"Child, let me worry about how I feel, and you just be at the house ready for a feast! Now, no more arguing...I feel my blood pressure rising," Jana relaxed back against her pillow and closed her eyes.

Noel stopped, afraid to upset Jana. John Wellings had to turn his back to keep from smiling as he could see right through his wife's 'high blood pressure.'

Noel truly wasn't worried about whether Jana could handle the company. She didn't have a problem cooking the entire meal for the family, bad cooking skills and all, but she didn't want to spend Christmas with Jesse and his new wife. Nausea washed over her in a steady stream at the thought, but for Jana, she would. Maybe this would be her pittance for running all those years ago. She'd have to watch the life she envisioned with Jesse from the side lines.

"Okay, I'll be there, but right now I have to go apartment shopping. I have an appointment in Mercer with a realtor in about 40 minutes. I'll stop back by this evening. Do you all need anything when I come back?"

"No dear. John's running out in a bit to get a shower and to pick up some things from the house. However, I'll be looking forward to that visit later. Maybe you can read some more Great Expectations to me after dinner. We are just getting to the good stuff."

Noel smiled, "I'd love that!"

Standing to her feet she leaned over and hugged the woman before she left, "I love you Momma Jay."

"Love you too sweetie. Good luck on the search for your new home." Jana's weak heart gave a gleeful leap at the thought of having her Noel back home once again.

Home. Noel liked the sound of that.

CHAPTER FORTY-TWO

Noel waited for Jimmy in the truck until his shift ended. She needed a few minutes alone to think about the options that were presented to her. All the apartments seemed wrong. Deep down she wanted to buy a home where she could build her life. She'd been living in apartments since college, and now she believed she was ready for a little more. The salary she'd been offered would certainly be enough to cover a decent home for her and a more dependable vehicle.

But…buying a home was such a huge step, and it'd take so much longer than the time she had. Jimmy had offered her a place to stay, but she didn't want to over-extend her welcome. He'd done so much for her already.

Maybe she needed a night to sleep on it.

"Hey," Jimmy said swinging the door open a huge grin on his face. "How was your day?"

She groaned and rolled her eyes.

"That good, eh?" He asked.

She sighed, "I don't know. I know I shouldn't complain. I mean, the realtor showed some nice places, but it just didn't feel like…"

"Home?" Jimmy asked putting the truck into reverse.

"Exactly," Noel said, relieved that Jimmy understood.

"Hmm, let me talk to a buddy of mine…you looking to buy or rent?"

He asked.

She paused for a moment really considering what she wanted, "I think I'd like to buy, but I do want to think on it for a day or two."

"Tell you what, I'll talk to my buddy just in case and see what he has, and if you change your mind—no harm no foul. I'm thinking time is of the essence, huh? I mean you have about a week and a half before you have to go back home, right?"

"Yes, originally I planned to go back before Christmas to start packing. I didn't think that Jana would want to have her annual Christmas dinner with the wedding and all but…"

Jimmy laughed, "You can't argue with that woman. For every ounce of kindness that is in her, there are two ounces of stubbornness."

Noel shook her head, "You're not wrong about that. Listen, do you mind stopping by the hospital for me to pop in really quickly? I told her I'd stop by."

"Yeah, no problem. I was thinking about grabbing some burgers from Mel's for dinner. How does that sound?"

"Fantastic! You can't have enough of Mel's. Just in case I haven't told you, I think you're pretty amazing." Noel grabbed his hand giving it a light squeeze.

"Amazing enough to date me?" Jimmy kidded. He didn't want to press the issue. Any man would be crazy to not fall head-over-heels in love with Noel, but her heart was elsewhere. Besides, he liked his girls a little ornerier than Noel could ever be. She was just too stinking nice for his taste.

"You really are impossible, you know that right?" She giggled..

"I think I've heard that a time or two." Jimmy laughed.

Pulling in front of the hospital, Jimmy let Noel out. "Just shoot me a text when you're ready, and I'll slide back by. I think Mel's due for a good harassing anyways."

"I will, thanks," Noel slid her tiny frame down from the truck. She thought of Mel and Jimmy and wondered what kind of shenanigans those two would come up with.

*   *   *

Jana was asleep, a half-eaten dinner tray on her bedside table. No one else was around, and Noel didn't want to wake her, so she sat by her side and rocked, closing her own eyes for a little rest.

She must've dozed off for a few minutes. She was shaken awake by Mr. Wellings.

"Noel?" He said in a hushed whisper.

"Pops? What's up? Is everything okay?" She asked, sleep heavy in her voice.

He waved his hands as if to ward off her thoughts, "Yes, everything's great. Can you follow me outside for a minute?"

Quietly, Noel grabbed her bag and followed Mr. Wellings out into the hallway. "What is it Pops?"

"Well, I had a talk with the doctor, and he thinks everything looks really good. Jana's blowing all the tests out of the water. He thinks she'll be ready to go home by Christmas Eve."

"That's great! Do you think she'll be up to it?" Noel asked.

Mr. Wellings nodded his head, but she could see reservation in his eyes. "Yes, I think she'll be fine as long as she isn't stressed about how the house looks for you kids during Christmas dinner."

Noel bit her thumb nail. "Shoot, I bet she'll stress about that. I can take care of the decorating. Is Marta around to help me?"

"Here's the thing," Mr. Wellings started. "Marta has her own family to spend time with although she's graciously agreed to pre-make our holiday meal."

"That's okay Pops. I can get it done. I'll start tomorrow." She wouldn't show her disappointment, but she'd have to cancel her last apartment viewing with her realtor.

Mr. Wellings smiled at the girl, "Jesse offered to help as well."

Noels body sagged, "I hate to sound like a child, but is he bringing Sara? Because if he is, I think it'd be easier if I decorated alone."

"Noooo…I believe Sara has other engagements this week with her family." Noel nodded her head, thinking Sara must be preparing for the last-minute wedding.

"I think Jesse and I can handle it., We helped Momma Jay enough when we were younger to know what to do." Noel agreed.

"That's fine. You have a key, and I'll let Jesse know you will be there tomorrow." Mr. Wellings said. He shifted nervously and avoided Noels eyes.

"You okay, Pops?" She asked.

"Oh yes, just tired. How about you go get some rest and start planning out how you want to decorate the house?" He gently put his hand on Noel's shoulders and directed her towards the elevator.

Noel giggled nervously, "Okay, tell Momma Jay I love her, and I'll swing by around lunchtime tomorrow if the snow holds off."

"Goodnight Noel. Be careful–those roads are slick." He said, still leading her away.

"I will. Jimmy's driving the truck, and he put chains on the tires, so I think we'll be good." Noel answered her brows wrinkled as she wondered why Pops was pushing her out.

"Fantastic, we'll see you tomorrow then!" With that, he escorted Noel into the elevator and rushed back to Jana's room.

"Okay?" Noel said punching the elevator button for the main level with her index finger. Pops was being super weird tonight. He probably needed a good night of sleep. Tomorrow she'd offer to stay with Jana, so he could get a good night's rest, but she was certain he'd refuse to leave her side.

What she wouldn't do for a love like that. Maybe one day, maybe one day.

*   *   *

Jana waited in the room for her husband to return. "Is she gone?" She asked in a whisper.

"Yes, I put her in the elevator myself. What happened to us not getting involved?" Her husband asked, kissing the top of his wife's deceptive head.

"Well, the pair of them are quite dim and may need a little push is all. I'm just getting them in the same room together. The rest is up to them. I won't interfere outside of that." Jana replied, a wide grin covering her pale face.

"Yeah, right," John growled.

"Why John Wellings! I'd never pry into the lives of those two children. But from time to time, a mother must help her babes come to the right conclusion with a little nudge is all."

John laughed at his wife. He was thankful she was still here with him and according to the doctors reports, she'd be with him for a while yet. And he couldn't disagree with his wife. He'd love nothing more than to see Noel and Jesse walk down the aisle one day.

"Now, just a few more things I'd like for you to make sure happens…just to help things a long dear."

John groaned, but sat at his wife's side as she laid out her master plan for the two unsuspecting young people.

CHAPTER FORTY-THREE

Looking around the shop, Jesse hoped an excuse to not help decorate the house would appear. His mother hated how he decorated., He never fluffed the tree branches enough, the Nutcracker dolls faced the wrong way, and apparently, he never quite got how to swirl the tree lights throughout the tree to make it shine brighter. Then there were the ornaments–he'd place them wherever he thought best, and she'd come along and completely rearrange them before she could fall asleep.

"You know I'm not good at that stuff, Pops," Jesse half whined to his father.

"Yeah, I told your mother that, and she suggested Noel help you. She always was a big help to your mother. She'll know how to set everything up the way momma likes it. You are mostly there for the heavy lifting," John said.

He was glad he was talking to his son over the phone or Jesse would've known something was up. John Wellings was a terrible liar.

"Pops, that's not a good idea. She left because of me, and now she's with Jimmy. I don't know if either one of us can handle it." Jesse said honestly.

"She agreed to do it," John answered.

"She did?" Jesse asked. "And she knows I'll be there?"

"Yes, she just wanted to make sure Sara wasn't around. Apparently, Noel doesn't know that you and Sara are no longer an item."

Jesse threw his head back, groaning loudly. "Alright, I'll do it, but if one of us ends up tied to the tree with Christmas lights you have yourself to blame Pops."

"Duly noted! She'll be there tomorrow afternoon. I left a list of things your mother would like done sitting on the dining room table."

"We'll get it done, I promise." Jesse said, wishing he could avoid Noel forever. At the same time, he couldn't wait to set eyes on her again. Maybe seeing her would keep him from staring at the painting he created of her for hours on end.

He needed to get it out of his office. That morning, he decided it'd be among the paintings going to New York for the spring gala at Yarma Zans. There were several pieces he'd be shipping up north that reminded him of her. Many of them would sell and some would come back home. He was okay with parting with them–all but one.

It was the painting she'd been standing near when she and Sara had their altercation. *Had she seen it? Did she know who the two children were sitting under the tree? Did she think of those days as much as he did?*

Their time together as children had been fun. Life with Noel had always been an adventure. She was full of joy and gave his life the spark he would've never known in her absence. He suspected she still could be adventurous. He knew one thing for sure–she kept him on his toes. And just as he thought when they were children, she was still the most beautiful girl he'd ever laid eyes on.

*   *   *

"And Jana wants you and Jesse to decorate the house, alone, together?" Jimmy asked over a steaming cup of black coffee.

"Yes," Noel said her porcelain cheeks turning a sweet shade of pink.

"Hmm," Jimmy sipped from his mug. That Jana was something else, but he liked what she was doing. If those two couldn't see how important they were to each other spending an evening alone sifting through old memories, then they were both idiots.

"What's hmm? What's that mean?" Noel asked suspiciously.

"Nothing princess, just hmm. Hmm, this is good coffee," he shook his head from side to side.

"Whatever, I'm going to bed. I'm thinking of doing something different for Jana. I want it to be special…I just don't know what to do yet." Noel stood and poured the rest of her decaf down the drain.

"Night. I think the roads are good, but if more snow falls, just take the truck in the morning. I am going to sleep in tomorrow. I have one day of rest before the mad house of last-minute, drugstore gift-buying begins. Since I don't have many plans for the holiday, I am taking the late shifts, but I will be off early enough to hang with you for your birthday."

Noel smiled at her friend. "You're a real saint, sir, a real saint."

Smugly Jimmy said, "Don't I know it doll, don't I know it!"

CHAPTER FORTY-FOUR

The next evening Noel stared at the closet, torn about what to wear. Part of her wanted to show up in sweats with a high ponytail, and part of her wanted to look so amazing Jesse's heart would thump out of his chest.

She chose the sweats and a high ponytail. There was no reason in the world to try and impress him. He'd likely not notice what she looked like anyway. Surely by now he was a bundle of nervous energy in anticipation of his upcoming nuptials.

Washing her face and slapping on some lotion, Noel looked at herself and decided she looked as good as she was going to that day. She did swipe on some baby pink lip gloss that looked perfect with her pale complexion, but that was it on the makeup front.

She was ready. Slipping into her car for the first time in a week, she started her engine. She'd miss the roar of her little muscle car, but she believed she was going find something a little more practical for traveling in the hills of her homeland.

The roads were nice and clear, but there was still plenty of snow on the ground. If the sun didn't melt it all away, she'd have a white Christmas. It had been a few years since she'd seen snow for Christmas, and she was giddy at the thought.

The night sky grew dark as she journeyed to the Wellings home. She took her time driving through town and decided to go the back way through the neighborhood where John and Jana lived. Their neighborhood was always among the best decorated when she was a child.

She wasn't disappointed in taking the scenic route. Every home was decked with lights and many had large inflatable yard decorations. A few of the homes even had snowmen gracing the lawns. She thought back to the many snowmen she and Jesse made over the years. When they were small, they'd pretend that every snowman they made was the same one come back for a visit year after year. Jana had bought a hat and scarf set she put back for them to use for Mr. Winters, as they called their annual frozen masterpiece.

Jesse's truck was in his parents' driveway, the house unlike the others in the neighborhood, dark and void of Christmas cheer. Her heart thudded, and her stomach seized up. *You can handle this, just get the job done for Momma Jay*, she thought.

"Jess? I'm here," Noel said, setting her purse on the kitchen counter.

Walking through the kitchen into the dining room, she saw he had started bringing tubs and totes of Christmas supplies out from the attic.

On the top of the totes sat a crate filled with Christmas records. The only time the family listened to the record player was during the holidays. Noel shuffled through the pile and snagged a Christmas jazz album. She loved the bluesy tunes that flowed so smoothly from the record player.

Noel closed her eyes, and memories of many years ago flooded her brain. If only she could go back in time to a simpler life, to a time when she and Jesse were still best friends; to a time when she didn't have a pain in her chest when she thought of him.

"Oh yeah, jazz!" Jesse said laying more boxes down. "Do you have any idea how many boxes of lights this woman has?"

Noel grinned, "I can only imagine."

Every year, Jana put weeks into decorating her home just as her neighbors did. It was an unspoken competition between the folks on their streets to see who could create the nicest light display.

"To be honest, it's a bit overwhelming. How in the world can we do what she did in just one night?" Jesse asked.

"I have an idea but it's going to take a little muscle and a lot of creativity." Noel answered.

"I'm listening," Jesse said, sitting on the couch.

"Well, remember that year Santa came here to visit because he missed my house?" She asked.

Jesse smiled thinking of that magical night. "I do," he said.

"Well, I want to recreate that magic for Momma Jay. I want to bring back those sweet memories and create some more."

He leaned forward, "What do you have in mind?"

"Here." She handed him a paper with some very crudely-drawn sketches of what she wanted to do.

Jesse looked up at her, his mouth smirked and brows shot halfway to his hairline. "Oh, shut it! We can't all be famous artists, Jesse Wellings."

He laughed, "I didn't say a word."

She held in her laugh long enough to chastise him, "You don't have to say anything, it's written all over your face!" Hands on hips she scolded him.

"What? It's not…bad!" He said.

"Thanks," she huffed.

"I mean the drawing is horrible, but the idea—not so bad…"

Noel grabbed a throw pillow and chucked it at his head. It bounced off his face and fell to the floor.

"Ouch, geez can't a man give his professional opinion–"

"Nope," Noel cut through him. "Let's get started. I'm sure you have plenty to do after you leave here."

In the snap of a finger, she had shut down and left the room.

Jesse's face fell. What happened? They'd been getting along just fine.

"Hey," Not wanting to be left out of her plans, he jumped to his feet. "What are you doing?"

"Looking for a flashlight." She shouted from the kitchen. "I want to see if the Santa sled is still in the workshop."

"It is. I'll get it. You start in here. Where do you want him?" Jesse asked.

Noel smiled wickedly, "On the roof."

Jesse rolled his eyes, "Of course you do!"

For the next several hours the pair worked diligently on the home, creating a beautiful winter wonderland that told the story of magic and love that Jana and John Wellings had shared with Noel and Jesse all their lives. Noel made it a point to work in the house while giving Jesse the heavy lifting chores outside. By eleven o'clock that evening the pair was bushed and not even close to being done.

"I can't go outside one more time tonight. My arms are sore from carrying that blasted sleigh up to the roof, and its fifty below out there. My fingers will literally fall off if subjected to the subzero temps one more time tonight." Jesse complained.

"It's not that cold, you baby," Noel opened the front door. "When did it start snowing?"

Jesse shook the snow from his hair, "Um, about an hour ago, I guess."

Noel drew her lips in a thin line, "I wonder what the roads are like?"

He shook his head, "It's probably not worth it to find out. We both have rooms here. Why don't we stay home and try to finish the rest of this stuff in the morning? I think I have most of the outside work done."

"Okay, let me call Jimmy so he doesn't worry, then I have to make some food. I forgot to eat dinner." Noel said, digging in her purse for her phone.

Sure, call Jimmy, he thought grudgingly. "How about frozen pizza? Momma keeps them in the freezer for me, like I'm still a teenager."

"Well, do you eat them?" She scrolled through her phone looking for Jimmy's number.

"Uh, yeah," Jesse said shaking his head. "It's pizza!"

Rolling her eyes, she called Jimmy. "Hey...yeah...I thought so too. Um, its...hold on let me go in the back..."

Offended she couldn't talk to her tall handsome bag of muscles in front of him, Jesse set to work. He started the oven and dug out a pizza stone banging it on the counter. Opening the fridge to find something cold to drink, he slammed the door after pulling out a bottle of lemonade from inside.

"What's with you?" Noel asked, watching his little fit from the dining room.

"Me? Nothing, I'm good!" He smiled and took a long pull of lemonade straight from the jug.

"Ugh, I'm gonna tell your momma you did that!" she said walking into the kitchen to find him a glass.

He shrugged, but hoped she didn't. Surgery or not, his momma would give him a whack if she found out he drank straight from the container.

"Did you let Sara know you weren't coming home? If she knows we're here together...alone...she may skin you alive." Noel taunted.

"I, uh, no...I didn't let Sara know..." Jesse's cheeks turned red.

Noel raised her eyebrows, waiting for an explanation as to why he wouldn't tell his soon-to-be wife he was staying the night in a home with a woman who had professed her undying love for him.

"I mean, I wouldn't like it if I were her," Noel pushed.

The oven beeped indicating it had preheated. "Good thing she's not you then, huh?" His words came out clipped and stung Noel.

"Yeah good thing. I'm going to take a shower while that cooks." Without waiting for a response, she turned on her heels and made for the bathroom.

She didn't have any clothes to change into, but she needed a minute away from Jesse. For some reason, they were both set on taking cheap shots at one another. *But why?* He'd moved on, or was he still upset she told him she wouldn't be his best man? Maybe it was time she found out. Staring at herself in the mirror, she abandoned the shower idea and decided to go straight to him.

When she was younger, she never held back how she felt with Jesse and here she was playing kid games trying to hurt him to prove a point. Stomping back through the house, she decided to tackle the problem head on.

He heard her approaching feet and couldn't help but smile. Oh, he knew she was mad, fuming. *Man was she gorgeous when she was angry,* he thought when she turned the corner to tell him off. Her nostrils flared, her cheeks blazed, and her eyes turned a smoky gray.

"What are you smiling about?" She asked, her chest heaving up and down.

Walking slowly towards her he ran the back of a hand down her cheek, "You silly."

"Humph," She grumbled pulling back. "Do I look like a clown to you, Jesse Wellings? Or how about a comedian? You want me to tell you a joke?"

He didn't even try to hide the laughter that broke across his face. "Noel," he stepped closer and leaned into her.

"Don't play all cute and innocent with me," she shoved her finger in his chest. "I'm tired of you acting like a baby. Stomping around, giving me and Jimmy death stares. Why I don't even know what we did for you to act like that."

"I give Jimmy death stares, not you," Jesse confirmed nonchalantly.

Noel jerked her head towards the ceiling, counting to three before responding. "But why? I thought you guys were friends."

"Friends don't move in on another man's…" Jesse stopped. Why was it hard to tell her how he really felt?

"Your *what* Jess? Old best friend from a different lifetime? You don't even know me anymore!" She shouted her raspy voice growing louder.

He took another step closer, his body touching hers. "I love you. I broke things off with Sara because I couldn't love her like I love you. And then to see you cozied up with Jimmy everywhere I turn. It's sickening. He's everything I'm not–rich, built like a bear, funny, and…"

"Built like a bear?" Noel asked her eyes widening. She wanted to laugh but she could see Jesse was dead serious.

"One day you tell me you love me, and the next you're living with the guy? I mean what the heck am I supposed to do here? And you're going back home in what like two weeks? Its agony knowing you're leaving, but even more knowing you are staying up Mountain Road with Jimmy Wren of all people. And for him, you will move back here, but for me…nothing."

Noel clasped her hands together then leaned her forehead on them. "I'm going to make some coffee. I think you and I have some catching up to do. Why don't you have a seat in the den, and I'll bring your pizza and some strong coffee?"

Great she was mothering him now, he wasn't a baby. But he did want someone to take care of him, and he knew he needed a minute to cool down.

He said, with as much dignity as he could muster, *"Fine."*

Noel bit her upper lip to maintain the seriousness of the situation, but she was having a hard time keeping her wits about her. Being an only child, Jesse could be a little spoiled., She noticed he hadn't grown out of that either.

She found the coffee and started a pot to brew. Coffee was nice, but she'd do anything for a cup of Jana's hot cocoa. Maybe with Christmas being just a few days away, Jana would share her secret with Noel.

Pulling the pizza out of the oven, Noel set it to cool while she waited for the coffee. Leaning against the counter, she shifted through their conversation. There was something he had said…something that she should have paid more attention to…

Did he say he broke off his engagement with Sara because he loved her?

Slinging the pizza on a serving tray, Noel made her way to the den. *Play it cool girl, play it cool,* she reminded herself.

CHAPTER FORTY-FIVE

An hour later. the pair were laughing like the old friends that they were—both light in spirit and full in their hearts. Noel sat in a chair across the room from Jesse. It was safer if they kept a distance for the time being. She nibbled on a piece of cold pizza crust, the coffee long gone.

"So, there's nothing going on with you and Jimmy?" Jesse asked in disbelief.

Noel shook her head, "Nope, we're just good friends."

"And you're moving back home just for the job and not to be with him?" He asked.

"I am," she smiled nodding her head. "My turn."

Jesse nodded his consent, "Go ahead."

"You and Sara are, like, over for real?" She asked.

"Yes, we never were a good match really. We met shortly after I saw you with some guy up at the University, and I gave up on tracking you down. You looked happy. The least I could do was let you live your life."

Noel shook her head, "I wish I had seen you there. But maybe things work out as they should. I mean surely Sara had good qualities that added to your life."

He shrugged. "She was a strong personality. She helped me build my business. It worked for a while but after I bought the engagement ring I thought about mom and dad. I thought about what they have, and I knew that Sara and I'd never be like that. I mean she's beautiful and business savvy but that's it. I think we would've been successful together and had an amazing looking life on the outside, but in my heart, I realized it wouldn't work."

"You realized all this after you bought her an engagement ring, after you planned for a Christmas wedding, on my birthday by the way," Noel shot his way.

Jesse looked sheepishly, "Sorry, I forgot about your birthday, but I think the kiss changed things for me. I didn't realize I could love someone like that. I had accepted that Sara and I'd just be okay, but then I kissed you, and it messed me up inside. I needed to get you out of my head by focusing on something else. I couldn't handle losing you again so I...I messed up. I'm stupid."

"But I saw you together at the hospital," Noel said confused.

"That was a bad moment, you kind of witnessed the tail end of the blow up. Basically, she figured out how I felt about you. She said she always knew, but with you so far away you were never a threat."

"How did she know?" Noel asked curious.

"My paintings, many of my early works were of me and you–after I saw you and Jimmy at the hospital, I kind of hate-painted you. When she went to clean out her desk, she saw the latest one..." He said.

"Hate-painted?" Noel asked, her eyes lighting up with curiosity.

"I was angry and painted you. It's nice actually–the painting I mean. I always paint better when I'm emotional."

"Like the one with the boy and the girl under the tree?" She asked.

"That's my favorite," he said.

"Mine too. Your work is amazing." Pride filled her chest thinking about how talented he was.

Jesse thought back to when they were younger, how she pushed him to do better with each painting, drawing, and sometimes sculpting–although that wasn't his niche.

"If it weren't for your encouragement, who knows what I'd be doing with my life? I know if you hadn't stood up for me our junior year and pushed dad to see my art for what it was, I may be running the pharmacy now."

"Well that wouldn't be the worst thing, but I'm glad you get to follow your dreams." Noel said.

"What about you? Are you following your dreams? "He asked.

Noel stared into the distance, thinking his question over for a moment. "Yes, I think I am. I want to change the lives of children. There were so many special teachers who looked out for me when I was a kid. If not for the help of those special educators and the love of one amazing family, I wouldn't have made it out of the world that threatened to overtake me."

Jesse felt a pang of guilt, "I wish I could go back in time–"

Noel shook her head, "Don't do that. I don't think I'd have pushed so hard to take care of myself if all that hadn't happened. My anger at you pushed me to work my way through college and to provide a home for myself. I had to prove I could make something of myself without you, without anyone."

"Well, I'm glad I'm good for something," he joked.

The chime of the grandfather clock in the hallway indicated that it was three a.m. "Oh my, it's so late. I know we have a lot more we need to talk about, but maybe we can save it for tomorrow?" Noel suggested.

His eyes drooped; sleep was ready to overtake him. "Sleep's a good idea." Standing to go to his room, he watched Noel as she gathered coffee cups and plates.

He could see it, her and him growing old together. Having children, maybe adopting a few. Christmas's just like the ones they shared as children. Smiling, he went to bed thinking of what the future could hold for them.

CHAPTER FORTY-SIX

A buzzing sensation above his head woke him from his slumber. Fumbling in the dark, he tried to find his phone. It took a few moments to find the device. "Hello," he answered groggily, dropping the phone twice before he placed it to his ear.

"Son?" Mr. Wellings asked. "Are you awake?"

"Yeah, yeah," Jesse ran his free hand over his face. "I'm up."

Mr. Wellings sighed. He knew better but didn't push the issue. "Momma's getting released this evening the doctor said."

"What! It's not Christmas Eve yet. We haven't finished getting the house ready." Jesse shot out of the bed.

Rushing down the hall in his boxer briefs, he swung Noel's door open. Covering the phone with his hand, he said, "Psst, hey Noel. Get up, get up!"

"Is Santa here?" She asked dumbly before slamming her pillow over her head.

Jesse hissed, pulling at the pillow. "Get up!"

"Jess you there?" His dad asked.

"Yeah, just um, just getting Noel up actually. The roads were bad last night so she stayed here."

Noel shifted in the bed as if to get up then pulled the lacy white comforter up to her chin and snuggled back into the bed. He tiptoed to her bed and shook her shoulder, "Get up, mom's coming home."

"What! Now?" Noel jumped from the bed, then stopped when she realized that Jesse had little clothing on.

Her eyes grew wide, "Um, you need clothes…I can't–go."

Looking down at his scantily clad body, Jesse ran from the room. "Jesse what's going on?"

"Sorry Pops, I'm here–it's okay…um, what time do you think she'll be released?" Jesse asked, running through his mind how he could possibly finished all they had left to do.

"Well the cardiologist wants to see her during his evening rounds and do some more labs. As long as everything comes back clear, he thinks we will be out of here around supper time." Mr. Wellings explained.

"Got it. Okay, Noel and I will have it done by then. Love ya, Pops. Call me if you need anything." Jesse said hanging up the phone.

Jesse threw on his pants and tossed on an old t-shirt from his chest of drawers. Making his way into the living room, he met Noel in the hallway. "You free today?" He asked.

"I definitely can be. I was supposed to look at apartments later today, but I can push it back." Noel said with a shrug. Her agent had been kind enough to allow her to move her appointments back a day, but she'd definitely not have time again before the holidays.

"You sure? I don't want you to miss out on finding a place." He replied.

"Yeah, Jimmy's supposed to hook me up with one of his buddies for a more permanent living arrangement." Noel said.

The pair walked to the kitchen where Noel started the coffee pot and Jesse pulled out eggs and popped some bread in the toaster.

"You looking to buy?" Jesse asked, happy to hear she was committed to come back home.

"I think so," she said pulling out mugs and creamer. "I mean, I know it'll be more work, but I think I can handle it."

"Nice! I hope you find what you're looking for." He said pulling out a skillet.

Noel reached for the skillet, willing to help with breakfast. He pulled back, "No way, last time you cooked in this kitchen mom had to remodel the entire room."

"Really? One little mistake and I'm labeled for life!" Noel tried to act offended, but she understood Jesse's hesitation. Truth be told, she had never learned how to cook much better since then.

They'd been about fourteen when she decided to microwave a packet of Pop Tarts. She thought the toasters made them too crumbly. The fire wouldn't have gotten so out of hand, but she had left the room and placed the entire aluminum packet in the appliance, then went outside to start her homework on the back deck.

Jana was so relieved that no one had died in the blaze she didn't get onto the kids much, but Noel carried guilt about the fire around for a long time. For weeks she tried to do work around the Wellings home to help cover the cost of the repairs, but the Wellings brushed her off.

Finally, Jana sat Noel down and confided in her, "Noel honey, I know you're upset by what happened, but truly I'm so thankful that you didn't get hurt. You learned a valuable lesson, and that's good enough for me." She lowered her voice so not to be heard. "And to be honest, I've been after John to remodel that kitchen forever. Now I get what I want!"

Jesse's voice brought her back, "Remember the fire of 93' do we?"

Chuckling, Noel nodded, "Yes, unfortunately I do, and I'm ashamed to say my cooking skills have not blossomed since that fateful day."

"Which is exactly why," he handed her a cup of the freshly brewed coffee, "I'm going to ask you to go relax in the dining room for a few moments, and I'll bring breakfast to you. Look at it as pay back for you waiting on me last night."

With a smug smile and a little shrug, Noel took her coffee and waited for her breakfast. Sitting at the dining room table, she wondered what a future with Jesse would be like. It was nice–the playful banter, reliving old memories, even if said memories were disastrous.

"Did Pops say what time Momma Jay was coming home?" Noel shouted to Jesse.

"He said around dinner time. They had some more tests to run and wanted to double check how she was doing before she comes home." Jesse explained.

"I'm glad she's doing so well." Noel said.

Jesse entered the room with two plates on his arm and the pot of coffee and empty cup in his other hand. "Yeah, everything happened so fast, and she wasn't getting better. When the doctor told us she may not survive the surgery...I almost lost it. I mean mom is what keeps this tiny family unit together. I don't know what Pops and I'd do without her."

Noel agreed, "Yes, she's pretty amazing. You're talented by the way. Do you have serving experience?"

"Are you kidding? I have to protect these hands!" Jesse sat the food down and held his smooth hands out for her to inspect.

"Mmm, nice. You better insure those things, you never know!" Noel said trying not to laugh.

"Joke's on you missy. I have insured these things. You know how clumsy I am!" Jesse raised his eyebrows at her. She wasn't sure he was serious or not about being insured but left it alone.

"Man, can you believe it's almost Christmas? What do you want from Santa this year?" Noel asked digging into her eggs.

Jesse paused for a minute watching Noel, her hair a mess, bags under her beautiful eyes, and he wondered, what do I want? *Her*. I want her for a lifetime and then some. I want to father her children and to spoil her beyond belief. I want to grow old and watch our grandchildren play in the yard.

He wanted to tell her those things but instead, he said. "I don't know. I haven't thought much about it. What about you?"

"You know a few weeks ago, I would've said something different but now...now I think I'd just like a home of my own. I've never really had that you know? I mean your family was great and provided so much–"

"But it wasn't *your* home." Jesse finished for her.

"Exactly, so if the big jolly man could find time to send me my dream home for Christmas, then I'd be grateful." Noel said finishing off her coffee. "Well let's get started, shall we?"

CHAPTER FORTY-SEVEN

Nine grueling hours later, Noel and Jesse laid haphazardly across the couch in the sitting room.

"Ugh, I stink," Noel groaned. "I stink, and I need fresh clothes and a shower."

"I may have some sweats and a sweater you can borrow," Jesse offered.

Noel shook her head, struggling to her feet. "I can't. Jimmy texted me earlier and said his friend has a few listings he wants to show this evening or else I will have to wait until I come back in February."

"Great, I hope you find what you're looking for," he said.

Tenderly looking at Jesse she thought, *I already have.* "Thanks, me too. I need to get going if I'm going to make myself presentable before I meet up with this guy. If I don't make it back tonight, tell Momma Jay I love her, and I'll be here tomorrow for a visit." Noel said.

"I will, see ya later." Jesse said.

"Later," Noel headed out the back door.

Popping to his feet, he watched Noel get in her beat-up Mustang and drive off. The talk they had the night before really helped close the gap from years past, but he couldn't help wondering if that'd be enough for them. *Only time would tell,* he thought, *at least she's moving back so the possibility of getting to know one another again would be there.*

*   *   *

The log home was quaint, yet skillfully built. Noel's jaw dropped as she pulled into the drive. Surely the realtor misunderstood. There was no way she'd be able to afford something this nice.

Getting out of her car, she approached Jimmy and his friend who met her at the home. "Are you sure this house is in my price range? I don't want to even step foot inside if I can't afford it."

Jimmy and his pal looked at one another, "Okay, it is a bit out of your price range, but the sellers are motivated to sell. I think you can get a great price for this property."

Noel groaned and rolled her eyes, "Jimmy," she said with warning in her voice.

"Hear him out, please," he tacked on the please after her murderous stare.

"Okay, there's a farmer on the back side of the land who is looking to expand his acreage. You could easily make up the difference by renting or selling a portion of the land to him." Jimmy's friend said.

Noel bit on her bottom, lip dying to see the inside of the home. "What's your name?" she asked giving in.

"Rich Miles," the man held out his hand to shake Noel's. Grudgingly, she grabbed his and gave him a firm handshake.

Once formalities were exchanged, Rich pointed to the home, "Shall we?"

Unable to conceal the grin that was creeping up her face, Noel led the way. When she walked inside the home, her heart dropped. It was perfect, it was beautiful, and she wanted it more than anything.

*   *   *

After a fitful night of sleep, Noel decided she had to see Jana and make sure she was doing okay. Filling a travel cup with coffee, she headed out the door with an overnight bag. Jimmy was already gone to the pharmacy and would spend most of Christmas Eve and Christmas day working. She left him a note asking for a rain check on the birthday celebration, so she could spend time with Jana before she went back to her apartment to prepare for her move.

Buying a house weighed heavily on her mind, and she was unsure of what to do. The only house she viewed the day before was perfect. She wanted that house more than anything, but she was afraid of not being able to afford it. What if the farmer changed his mind? What if some major repair came up? Crunching numbers, she knew she could do it, but things would be tight for a few years. She'd been looking forward to the financial stability her new position would provide.

Disappointed, she decided she needed to wait on buying her dream home. There were just too many unknown factors in her life. It'd make someone a beautiful home one day.

CHAPTER FORTY-EIGHT

"Pops? Momma Jay? Is anyone here?" Noel walked through the quiet home.

Mr. Wellings called from the den, "Back here kiddo."

Noel followed his voice and found a smiling Mr. Wellings and a crying Jana.

"Momma Jay? What's wrong?" Noel kneeled next to the woman.

The woman looked pitiful. She was tightly cocooned in an old Afghan and had a pile of used tissues scattered around her while a half-empty box of Kleenex sat on her lap.

"Don't mind me sweetie. I'm just overwhelmed a little. There are so many things that I would like to do for Christmas, but I don't think I have the energy for it all." Jana smiled gratefully at the girl. "The decorating you and Jesse did here is just magnificent. I love it so much. The displays bring back so many beautiful memories. Thank you."

"Well there's more to it, but you have to wait until tomorrow to see," Noel said a hint of mystery in her voice.

"You're the sweetest child. Lord knows I needed you in my life." Jana ran her hand over the girl's head.

"Is Jesse here?" Noel asked.

"No, he had to run to the pharmacy to grab a prescription for me. He called a few minutes ago to say he may not make it back until late this evening. Said he had some business to attend to and he needed to stop at the gallery."

"Cool," Noel tried to mask her disappointment. She wondered if he wanted to see her as bad as she wanted to see him. "What can I do to help get ready for tomorrow?"

"Well, you know it wouldn't be Christmas without my Gingerbread cookies...would you mind making a few batches? I'll even lend you my recipe." Jana offered.

"I'd love to, if you trust me in your kitchen again..."

Jana chuckled, "I'll have John unplug the microwave. Besides I'm sure you've learned to cook by now."

Noel made a face, *that's what you think*. "Ha-ha little lady, of course I'll make them. Now tell me where's the secret vault filled with all your yummy recipes?"

* * *

It was nine that night before Jesse made it back to the Wellings' home. He had a busy day planned and it had gotten even busier once he decided on the perfect gift for Noel and his family. He only hoped that it wouldn't scare her off.

The scent of burnt gingerbread hit his nose as he opened the back door, a groan of despair wailed from the kitchen. He knew the cry well. Fixing his face so he wouldn't upset her, he walked into the house.

Sure enough, Noel sat in the kitchen with three dozen burnt gingerbread men on the counter. "Need some help?" He asked.

"Thank God, yes, how does she do it? I've burnt every single cookie I've made. If there is a Christmas hell, this is it!" Noel's eyes sparkled with tears of frustration.

"Here, let's scrap these guys and work together. I just want to check on momma."

"Okay," she sniffled. "They went to sleep early; Momma Jay wore herself out today, I think."

"Okay, I'll just poke my head in. Then we'll make some cookies," Jesse walked from the room. Noel watched his retreating back until he was gone.

Bowing her head in relief, Noel relaxed. She'd been so disappointed that she burnt all the cookies. Baking had never been her thing, but she'd tried so hard to follow Jana's recipe. It was her first Christmas back in years. She wanted to make everything perfect just as Jana had done for them all those years.

"You ready to get our bake on?" Jesse asked coming back in the room. He looked tired.

"Rough day?" She asked.

"No, just long. I'm happy to see you here." Jesse said, heat climbing up his face. Why was it so hard to talk to her?

She too turned red and busied herself cleaning the burnt mess she'd created. "Me too. Thanks for helping me. I've no idea what I'm doing here, and I really just want everything to be perfect."

Jesse walked behind her and massaged her shoulders. "Everything *will* be perfect. We'll all be together and that's all that matters. Hey...," he turned her around to face him when he heard her sniffling.

She gulped loudly, "I know...I just...I feel so guilty about everything," and there it was—the crumpled, red face and jittery jaw. The ugly girl cry. The most dreaded face a woman could have in front of a man she loved.

He pulled her close and ran his hands up and down her back as she let out days, months, maybe even years of guilt out in body-rocking sobs. "It's okay, you're just stressed. You have a lot on your plate. Just take a deep breath and repeat after me...this is all temporary...things are getting better..."

Sniffling, she nodded, snot flowing from her nose as quick as the tears. "This is all temporary.... things are getting better..."

He nodded holding her at arm's length, "Okay one more—"

She smiled at his kind eyes, the way his nose crinkled slightly when he spoke, and the devilish way his mouth turned up when he was up to no good—just as he did now.

"This one is important..." Narrowing her eyes on him, she knew he couldn't be trusted. "I should never cook ever again...like seriously ever again."

Slapping his shoulder, "Oh stop!"

"Ouch!" He laughed, then scooped her back in his arms hugging her tight to him. There was an undeniable comfort feeling the warmth of her body against him.

Pulling back, his eyes grew serious and hers grew wide. Both were scared the rapid beating of their hearts could be heard in the room that had suddenly grown too quiet. Slowly, Jesse bent his head and grazed her lips with his. She gasped at his touch. This kiss was different than the last.

The passion that he had displayed last time was still there but also there was a gentleness she'd never experienced. From the tips of her toes to the top of her head, she felt love grow inside her and pulse from her body ready to burst at the seams.

It lasted only seconds, but it was enough...enough for both of them to see...

"Good night Irene, what is it with you two? Every time I see the two of you together, you are locking lips!" Marta said busting through the back door and into the kitchen.

"Marta," Jesse said pulling back. "What are you doing here so late? I thought you had already prepared everything."

"Mrs. W called me earlier this evening and asked me to make some gingerbread cookies. Said she could smell the burnt gingerbread all the way back in her room." Marta puckered her lips and looked Noel up and down. "Looks like cookies ain't the only thing on fire in here. Mmmhmmm."

Noel and Jesse looked at one another, both cheeks ablaze. "Marta," Noel started.

"No need to explain to me girlie, you know how I feel about the two of you. I'm just glad you came to your senses. Well, I'll be off, there's icing in that bowl there. You two can keep your hands busy icing them cookies...Merry Christmas." She smiled sneakily, and in a flash, as was typical for the woman, Marta was gone.

"Well, maybe she's right...we should–"Jesse started.

Getting to work right away, Noel agreed, "Yup, cookies it is."

*   *   *

Noel woke with a start confused to where she was for a moment. The white lace comforter that tangled itself around her body reminded her of where she was. Then she remembered it was Christmas Day, and she bounded out of the bed.

Christmas morning was always special at the Wellings', Santa came in the wee hours of the morning delivering gifts to all. It didn't matter that they were adults. Santa always came Christmas morning. Puttering down the hall, Noel peeked into the family room where she heard the whispers of Mr. and Mrs. Wellings.

"Oh, there she is, Merry Christmas!" Jana called out. Noel noticed her color looked much better than it had since coming home from the hospital.

Sleepily, they looked at one another. The presents were under the tree, but Jesse was nowhere to be seen.

"If Jesse's not here, do I get his presents?" Noel asked looking around the room. She was disappointed Jesse wasn't with them.

The Wellings both laughed, remembering years past when the kids would try anything to steal a present from the other. After the 'Year of Santa' as Noel and Jesse called it–the year the Wellings staged his visit–Noel was treated just as Jesse on Christmas morning. They had the same amount of presents and were treated as equals in the eyes of John Wellings' pocketbook.

Jana looked to her husband before answering Noel. "I know normally we'd open gifts Christmas morning, however, Jesse asked we do something a little different this year. He wants us to wait for our presents until after dinner...he said he has a surprise for us. And apparently his surprise will keep him from joining us until dinnertime."

John wrapped an arm around his wife. Jana didn't like changing her Christmas Day traditions.

"What could he possibly be doing?" Noel asked more to herself. Except for the pharmacy, most of Old Harmony shut down for Christmas.

"I'd like to know that as well. If it's not for a good reason, Jesse Wellings will have some serious making up to do." Jana answered in a huff.

"Okay...well what do we do then? You want me to make breakfast?" Noel asked.

"No!" Both Mr. and Mrs. Wellings shouted at the same time.

"Okay, okay, sheesh, I get it I'm a terrible cook...Um...I can see if Mel's is open and get something to go." she suggested.

Mr. Wellings shook his head. "No, I saw Mel yesterday. She told me she was closed down for the day. Said something about cooking for ungrateful kids..."

Noel sighed. Mel complained about her kids all the time. Everyone knew she secretly loved cooking for them and spoiling them when she could, even if they were grown.

"Well dear, if it's not too much trouble there's a tiny breakfast place on the other side of Mercer that has some amazing crepes, and I happen to know the woman who runs the place is Buddhist, so she should be open...it's a bit of a drive I'm afraid." Jana looked at Noel with puppy eyes, and she had to wonder what the woman was up to, but she quickly agreed.

"Okay, I can do that. Let me change, and you and Pops write down what you want, and I need an address."

"Sure thing dear," Jana quipped with a smile.

Noel shook her head. Jana was definitely up to something. However, Noel was willing to wait it out. Jana always gave the best surprises.

*   *   *

She had no choice. After driving around lost for thirty minutes, Noel pulled over and called Jana. She took a few deep breaths to shake off the frustration she felt from driving around on Christmas morning for crepes.

"Hello dear, are you okay?" Jana asked loudly.

"Jana, my GPS isn't pulling the restaurant up. Are you sure about the address?" Noel asked.

"I'm sure dear, 1008 Wrights Mill road...I've been there dozens of times."

Noel slumped in her seat, "Oh no, you wrote 8001 Wrights Mill Road."

"Did I? I'm so sorry sweetie...it must be these meds making me out of sorts. I'm so sorry...I'll tell you what, I'm sure I have some cream of wheat or something in the kitchen dear, you come on back home." Jana apologized.

Guilt filled Noel's gut, it was Christmas and Jana's heart was set on crepes. How many times had the woman provided meals for her? "No, I can't be far now. I'll...I'll get them and be home in no time."

"You're an angel," Jana said. "See you soon," then the line went dead.

Letting loose an annoyed breath of air, Noel punched in the right address in her GPS and headed in the opposite direction.

Twenty-five minutes later, Noel reached her destination. Her heart sank when she pulled into the parking lot. The place was packed. People stood out the door in a line. "Good thing I love you so much Momma Jay," Noel said to herself.

Turning her car off and zipping up her jacket for the wait to get inside, Noel hopped out of her car to brave the cold and the crowd.

CHAPTER FORTY-NINE

"How long do we have?" Jesse asked, carefully carrying the canvas inside. It was his gift to her, well part of her gift.

"Well Josephine's is the only place open for miles. I'm sure by now they'll be packed. I'd say we have maybe an hour and a half, tops...I do hate lying to her, especially on Christmas." Jana said with a pout.

"I know what you're doing, and it's not going to work on me. I will not tell you what I have planned. It's gonna be worth it–that's all you need to know. However, I am going to need way more time than an hour and a half to pull this off." Jesse said seeing through his mom's pitiful act.

"This surprise better be good young man!" With a gleam in her eyes, she gave him the mom stare, and she meant it.

"I promise," Jesse said planting a kiss on his mother's cool cheek. "I gotta go. Can you do me one more favor and call Jimmy...I'm going to need his help."

"What do I need to do?" Jana asked conspiratorially.

Jesse grinned wickedly and shared his plan with his mother.

*   *   *

Just as she finished placing her order of three meals of blueberry crepes and bacon, Jimmy called.

"Hello?" She answered.

Jimmy's voice burst through the tiny speaker, "Noel? You busy?"

"Um, kind of...what's up?" She asked.

"Crazy thing, my brother was checking the Christmas lights on his roof...and he fell off the ladder...he's okay except maybe for a broken arm. Jackie has the baby and he's sick, so it'd be rough on them to take him out in the cool weather and all. So, I will need to take my brother to the hospital. I called in Jeff, the new guy, but could you come help him just show people where things are? It's a zoo in here, and I don't know what to do. Jeff can handle the registers and everything..." Jimmy begged.

"I mean, I'm in Mercer getting Jana some food...I don't..." Noel trailed off. She hated telling Jimmy no; he had done so much for her. Dang these people always making her feel guilty.

"Jared lives in the same neighborhood as the Wellings. If you bring the food here I can stop it to them on my way." Jimmy waited expectantly for an answer.

Noel sighed. She rarely told people no. More than anything, she wanted to eat breakfast with the Wellings, spend time with Jesse, and enjoy the holiday she loves the most, but Jimmy had gone above and beyond for her.

"Sure, I'll help you. I'll be there as soon as I can. Give me about twenty-five minutes. I hope your brother is ok."

Jimmy sighed in relief, "You're the best. What would I do without you?"

"I honestly have no idea! See ya in a few." Noel said. Some Christmas this was turning out to be.

"See ya," Jimmy said and hung up. "Whatever you're up to Wellings had better be fan-freaking-tastic." He added to himself, hoping whatever Jesse had planned would be amazing.

CHAPTER FIFTY

It was six o'clock and no sign of Jimmy. Noel's feet throbbed. She hadn't worn proper shoes for a day in the pharmacy. Cute winter boots looked amazing but wreaked havoc on the toes.

"Jimmy said we can close at six, so you're free to go." Jeff said waving her goodbye.

"Okay...thanks. Merry Christmas, Jeff," Noel said, rushing off before the pharmacy received another rush of last-minute shoppers. Shoppers ready to bombard the place for last minute gift cards and candy, shoppers who wanted to linger in the store instead of braving the bitter cold.

"Merry Christmas," was Jeff's reply.

Stepping into the crisp winter air, Noel pulled in a deep breath and hopped into her little car.

Darkness had taken over the sky indicating the day was coming to an end. Noel was slightly upset she'd missed the day with the Wellings. She'd so badly wanted the day to be perfect. She should've known better, she chastised. In her world, things rarely worked out as they should.

Pulling into the driveway, Noel noticed that the Wellings' home looked dark. Many of the displays and lights that she and Jesse had hung were turned off... and some were even missing!

Confused, she quickly got out of her car and walked to the house. Her confusion grew when she opened the kitchen door to a semi dark room. The only lights that were on were Christmas lights forming a path that led from the room into the dining area.

Standing in the middle of the kitchen, looking incredibly handsome in a dark sweater and custom fit jeans stood Jesse. He shifted uncomfortably.

Tilting her head to one side while absently placing her purse down on the counter, she asked, "What's this?"

He chose not to answer her question. Instead he walked to her and pulled her hands in his. "Merry Christmas, Noel. I hope this gift will make up for the day you've had."

"It's okay., It's not like it was your fault that I was stuck in the pharmacy all day long." Noel said.

"Actually it was," Jesse confessed. "I do hope you will forgive me, but I put Jimmy up to calling you in for help. I needed time to do a few things…for you."

Cocking her head to one side, Noel's lips moved slightly up her face. "I don't understand what you mean. Jimmy's brother got hurt, and he asked me to help so he could take him to the hospital."

Jesse sighed, "It's a long story, but I asked Jimmy to lie to you so I could do something special for you." She opened her mouth to lay into him good. Holding up his hand to silence her, Jesse said quickly, "Give me a few moments and if you still want to yell at me, feel free, but first–I have all these things I want to say to you, but it may take me a little while. My stomach is tied in knots and the words that I need to say are all jumbled in my brain. Tonight, instead of me fumbling my words, I want to show you how I feel if you'll let me. Will you allow me to escort you this evening?"

Suddenly self-conscious in her old clothes, with no makeup, and frazzled hair, Noel nodded.

"Take my arm," he held his elbow out for her to take.

He led her into the dining room. Just feet into the room, he stopped. Tears filled her eyes as she saw what he'd done. Standing in front of a canvas, Jesse said, "The day I first sketched this, it felt we had been best friends forever, although it had really only been a few years.". Drawing you that day was the first time I realized how beautiful you were. Even then…"

She released his arm and walked to the painting...a replica of the first picture he'd drawn of her. The one he had gifted her on her birthday, *the year of Santa.*

The painting had so much more depth than the original drawing and captured her likeness as a child perfectly. He had even added the window and the silhouette of Santa flying across the moon as he had done so many years prior in the sketch.

"I still have the original, it's a little wrinkled but much loved." She said tears glistening in her eyes.

"There's more," he said pointing to path of lights leading into the sitting room.

Eager to see what else he had in store, Noel followed the path. In the sitting room sat another painting. This picture made her smile. It was the one of her and Jesse under the big oak in his parents' back yard. "I love this one." She touched it lightly with her fingertips then pulled away. She knew she shouldn't touch it with her bare skin.

He was such a talented artist; the painting took her back to the days when they were kids and would sit for hours under that tree. Usually she was coming up with some wild idea that would get them nearly killed, and he was the voice of reason talking her off the ledge.

"*Are there more*, she asked?" Jesse said mysteriously, then nodded and pointed to where the path of lights led.

She followed the path and stopped at the next painting. This one she hadn't seen but it was of what she looked like now. She looked at him with question in her eyes. "The hate picture?"

He chuckled, "Yeah. All I wanted to do was paint...to get lost in it, to forget you, instead this happened."

She smiled. He too was on her mind no matter how hard she tried not to think of him. She was grateful she couldn't paint, or his face would have been plastered all over her apartment.

She loved the painting. It was painted in shades of black, grey and white, but it captured every single detail of her face. How could he remember those details enough to paint them?

This time she didn't ask; she just followed the lights to the den. There in front of the Christmas tree on a gold easel displayed a painting that didn't quite make sense.

It was a painting of a man and a woman holding each other, their backs were to the audience, but she had a feeling she knew who they were. The woman had her head leaned on the man's shoulder and he had his arm wrapped around hers. They looked at a beautiful log home, a home she had seen before. A home she wanted desperately to be her own.

"How do you know of this place?" she glanced at Jess then looked back at the painting. She hadn't had a chance to tell him about the home–how could he have possibly known?

Turning back to face him, she gasped. "What are you doing?"

He was on one knee. A ring, a beautiful, diamond engagement ring was pinched between his fingers. He held the ring delicately in the air as if it were the most precious item in the world. She covered her face with her hands but kept her eyes free to take in Jesse and his words.

"I missed my chance with you years ago, and I don't want to make that mistake again. You can turn me down. I don't blame you if you do, but Noel, it's always been you...I was so scared, I almost made a horrible mistake with the wrong woman and that would have wrecked many of our lives. When I kissed you the first time, I knew I never wanted to feel what not holding you in my arms felt like again. I assumed a great many things, that you hated me, that I could move on, and that you loved Jimmy. I sulked and acted like a child...now I sit here begging you to forgive me for being so stupid, for not seeing right away what you meant to me. Today, Noel Miracle, I ask you on your birthday, on our favorite holiday of all, will you allow me to be your best friend for life? Will you allow me to be your husband? And will you allow me to gift you with your own home? Please say yes, I don't want to live in that big house all alone..."

Tears coursed down her face, she was at a loss for words. What had he done? What was he saying? He had bought her dream home?

She shook her head, she tried to mouth the words, but no sound would come out.

Frightened of her reaction, Jesse's arms drooped. Would she refuse him? Had he been too late? Maybe she'd never be able to get over the past.

Noel stooped to her knees and looked Jesse in the eyes. She took a shaky breath and said, "I've dreamt of this day since high school. I've imagined marrying you, having children with you, for once in my life having a real home–with you. I tried to move on with my life as well, but no one could compare to you. Last night when you kissed me, it was like a small glimpse into the future."

"Is that a yes..." Jesse asked expectantly. His hands shook and grew clammy.

Closing her eyes, she imagined a life without him. It was a thought she couldn't bear.

"We would have to get to know each other again…" she said. This was crazy. They hardly knew each other anymore.

"We'd have forever." he answered.

"And I don't want to live together until after the wedding, which could be a while…"

"Take the house and make it our home, I'm patient. Just give me a small glimmer of hope that one day you will be my wife." He said.

"You're making it hard to say no," she smiled.

"Then don't," he grabbed her hand and slid the ring just around the tip of her ring finger.

"Okay," she nodded, tears leaking from her eyes. "Yes, I will marry you!"

Jana's voice shook from behind, as she clapped her hands. "Oh thank the Lord!"

Jana hobbled to the couple and wrapped her arms around Noel and Jesse sobbing tears of joy. "Now you really will be my daughter! The Lord has been so good to us!"

"Yes, He has," Noel conceded. She pulled the woman close to her and Jesse.

"Sorry Jana. We had another surprise for you, but it looks like some of our lights came up missing." Noel glanced at Jesse.

Looking sheepish, he looked around the room. "About that…I needed the lights for this," he pointed to the lights he created for Noel's path of paintings.

"You're forgiven," Noel grabbed both sides of his face and kissed him on the mouth. "Now, who's hungry? My stomach is eating on my backbone!"

Jesse rolled his eyes and groaned, "How about I warm dinner up and you keep momma company? Pops, what do you say to helping me with dinner this year?"

Mr. Wellings smiled, "I think that would be a fantastic idea."

Both men kissed their ladies and scampered off to make the holiday meal. Noel snuggled next to Jana and laid her head on the woman's shoulder.

"Is it silly?" Noel asked holding her ring at arm's length admiring its sheen. It was a beautiful band, she was glad it wasn't as flashy as the one he had shown her before. She liked things simple and plain.

"Is what silly, dear?" Jana asked as she too gazed at the sparkling diamond that adorned Noel tiny finger.

"I mean, just days ago Jesse and Sara were together. Jimmy and I were almost a thing. Is it all too much, too fast?" Noel asked.

Jana waved her hand in the air, "So goes life. Love works in strange ways, but I will say this—when you find love, lose it, and it comes back to you—honey don't let it go! From the moment you came back home, Jesse's had eyes for you only. If he were honest, he'd admit that he never stopped loving you, he just lost hope. Besides, take it from me. Life is way too short to worry about all that nonsense when you have the love of your life right in front of you."

"I never stopped loving him, but I kind of feel bad for Sara, ya know?" Noel admitted a ball of guilt settling in her belly.

"I have a feeling Sara Rhymes will move on just fine. Don't worry about her, worry about the wedding and this fancy new house you have to decorate. Your new home."

Home, Noel smiled. She had never felt like she had a real home before and here it was offered to her on a silver platter by the man of her dreams. There were still a great many things to work through with Jesse, but she knew that no matter what they'd make it through the trials of life together just as they had when they were young.

CHAPTER FIFTY-ONE

Five Years Later

The tree lighting ceremony was soon, and Noel hoped she could hold out long enough to see it. No matter how she felt, she was determined to make it to the celebration and get some of Momma Jay's fresh baked cookies and famous hot cocoa. She had been craving them for days.

"You doing okay?" Jesse asked wrapping his arms around her from behind.

"Mmm, yes. I'll be doing better when I get my hands on some cookies." Noel whined.

Jesse kissed her neck then spun her around to face him. "I've received word that there is a special package waiting for you over at Mom and Pop's booth, special for a party of three."

"That's a shame," Noel smiled wickedly.

"What?" Jesse asked puzzled.

Noel's grin grew, "That there's only enough cookies for me and little man here." She rubbed her belly, eager to see their bundle of joy.

"Them's fighting words, lady," Jesse growled.

"Do you wanna go there with me, Mr. Wellings?" She asked her brows shooting up her forehead. Baby cravings were no joking matter.

"No, madam!" he said ducking his head and lifting his arms in surrender.

"Hey look, is that Jimmy over there? Let's go say hi, we haven't seen in in ages."

"Looks like he's on a date," Jesse said holding back. He still felt weird being around Jimmy after how awful he acted when he and Noel hung out.

Noel squinted. He was holding hands with a woman. She had her back to them however, and Noel couldn't tell who she was. The way the woman held herself seemed familiar, but Noel wasn't sure why.

"Let's go say hi anyway. He'd be upset if we didn't." Noel grabbed her husband's hand and led him over to the large man and the woman he now had wrapped in his enormous arms.

"Hey you," Noel said loudly to be heard over the crowd.

Turning to them Jimmy smiled and released the woman he was holding and squeezed Jesse and Noel in his embrace. "Man, I haven't seen you all since when? This summer? You ain't using the pharmacy across town, are you?" He pulled back looking at the pair sternly.

"Oh hush," Noel swatted him. "As if we'd ever sell out to the large corporate pharmaceutical biz when we have Wren's Pharmacy right here," Noel smiled. She had heard he finally changed the name of the pharmacy from Wellings' to Wren's during the summer.

"We've been busy preparing the nursery," Noel said patting her giant belly.

"Oh yeah, what are ya having?" He asked his eyes looking down at her baby bump.

"A boy," Jesse said with a proud swagger.

"A boy, how about that! I hope one day to have a few myself, now that I've settled down. I guess now is as good a time as any," Jimmy pulled the woman from behind him forward.

Jesse and Noel stood in shocked silence, mouths dropped open in complete shock. The woman he introduced was none other than Sara Rhymes.

"Uh, this may be a little awkward, but meet Sara...we um, we're going to be married soon." Jimmy said his cheeks turning red. Through her shock, Noel wasn't surprised. Jimmy always had liked the tough girls.

Sara looked at Noel and Jesse hanging back just a little. Noel noticed she seemed softer, her face less severe. "Hi," Noel said brightly.

Sara smiled at Noel but just looked at Jesse. "Congratulations," she said looking down at the ginormous lump attached to Noel's front.

"Thank you," Noel said. Jesse shifted uncomfortably in his coat.

"Well, we have to go. If I don't get some cookies in my belly soon I don't know what may happen." Noel said.

"You better bring that baby in to see me!" Jimmy said, giving Noel one last hug.

Noel saluted, "Yes, sir! See you later!"

Once out of earshot, Jesse said, "That was a little tense wasn't it?"

Noel shrugged, "Nah not too bad, Sara seemed a little more laid back than she was before. I'm sure Jimmy has a lot to do with that. He's a good guy." Noel laughed, "She'll certainly keep him in his place."

Jesse nodded his head, "I'm sure she will." Jesse hugged and kissed his wife. "I am the luckiest man alive, and I don't much care what happens with anyone but me and you." He pulled something from his pocket. It was a box, bigger than a ring box but not by much.

"What is this?" she asked, pulling off the tiny red bow that was tied around the black satin box.

He shrugged, "A gift from Santa."

Pulling the lid back, she studied the item in the box. It took her several seconds to make sense of it all, but finally she got it and laughed as tears of love came to her eyes.

"It's beautiful!" She exclaimed as she put the bracelet around her wrist, "Here, clasp it for me," she said.

Once the silver bracelet was fastened tightly she continued to study each and every single item on the charm bracelet. There was a diamond-encrusted snake, a paint brush, a Christmas tree, a baby rattle, a tiny log home, a charm with a boy and a girl eating what looked like popsicles, and a tiny oak tree, but her favorite was a tiny picture frame with a miniature replica of the painting he made of them together in front of their little dream home.

"Dang your hide, Jesse Wellings. You're making me cry!" She said kissing his face over and over.

"Only tears of joy I hope?" He asked looking at his beautiful bride.

"Yes," she agreed. Looking at the man she fell in love with many years ago she wondered how much more she could love him. Her gaze moved down to her belly, and a tiny kick rocked her stomach. Feeling the life they created there, she knew the answer to that question to be more than she could ever imagine.

Grabbing his hand, she led him to where her mother-in-law waited to shower her son and new daughter with love and of course, chocolate chip cookies.

ABOUT THE AUTHOR

Rachel was born and raised in Hardin County, Kentucky. She loves spending time learning new things and is an avid hobby collector. Rachel loves spending time with her three beautiful daughters and awesome husband. She adores chocolate and is obsessed with all things Harry Potter. To learn more about Rachel and to connect with her on social media click on the links below.

https://www.facebook.com/RachelRenayLopez
https://www.instagram.com/rachelrenaylopez/
https://twitter.com/rachel_r_lopez
https://rachelrlopez.com/

OTHER BOOKS BY RACHEL LOPEZ

The Water Cave: Book One in the Transporter Series
The Cave of Darkness: Book Two in the Transporter Series

COMING SOON

The Fire Cave: Book Three of the Transporter Series
Jackson's Song